The pounding rhythm—the chanting, the keening—started once more in Skye's mind

There was another decision to make. Was the officer lying on the concrete floor yet another fallen hero she needed to help to the other side?

She took the man's hand and a sensation pulsed through her, startling her. There was something this officer had left to accomplish—needed to accomplish. Something utterly critical yet to come in his future. Something important to her? A bond of some kind between them?

She sensed some intense emotions inside his mind as well as a determination to survive.

The cop could not die.

You will live. It is not yet your time. Open your eyes. The unspoken voice was hers, and it was inundating him with a life force that flowed intentionally, excruciatingly, from her.

Officer Owens groaned and opened his eyes. They were dark, the deep brown of polished mahogany, and stared straight into Skye's.

He was going to live.

Books by Linda O. Johnston

Silhouette Nocturne

Alpha Wolf #56
Back to Life #66

LINDA O. JOHNSTON

first made her appearance in print in *Ellery Queen's Mystery Magazine* and won the Robert L. Fish Memorial Award for Best First Mystery Short Story of the Year. Now, several published short stories and many novels later, Linda is recognized for her outstanding work in the romance genre.

A practicing attorney, Linda enjoys juggling her busy schedule of writing contracts and other legalese, along with creating memorable tales of the paranormal, time travel, mystery, and contemporary and romantic suspense. Armed with an undergraduate degree in journalism with an advertising emphasis from Pennsylvania State University, Linda began her versatile writing career running a small newspaper, then working in advertising and public relations and later obtaining her J.D. degree from Duquesne University School of Law in Pittsburgh.

Linda belongs to Mystery Writers of America and Sisters in Crime, and is actively involved with Romance Writers of America, participating in the Los Angeles and Orange County chapters. She lives near Universal Studios, Hollywood, with her husband and two Cavalier King Charles spaniels.

Back to Life

LINDA O. JOHNSTON

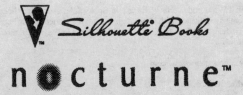

Silhouette Books

n●cturne™

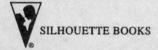 SILHOUETTE BOOKS

ISBN-13: 978-0-373-61813-2

Recycling programs
for this product may
not exist in your area.

BACK TO LIFE

www.silhouettenocturne.com

Printed in U.S.A.

Dear Reader,

A few years ago, I was fortunate enough to take a Baltic Sea cruise. I visited several Scandinavian countries, and was interested to see that very little today spoke of the fascinating legends of their past. I started doing research on my own—and *Back to Life* was the result!

Nordic legends abound with stories involving Valkyries—a term evolved from an old Norse word meaning "choosers of the slain." In some tales, Valkyries are terrible, ugly creatures that cause death. In others, they are lovely, virginal women who decide which mortally wounded warriors are worthy of saving for future battles, and whisk them to a wonderful afterlife in Valhalla. I liked the latter idea, although the Valkyries in my mind were real women with sexual urges they could fulfill.

In *Back to Life*, Skye Rydell, a K-9 cop, is the descendant of generations of Valkyrie women with the power of deciding, in many situations, who will live and who, if dying, will cross a rainbow bridge and face a peaceful afterlife. When she makes a split-second decision to save the life of mortally wounded SWAT officer Trevor Owens, her life is changed forever.

I hope you enjoy it! Please come visit me at my Web site: www.LindaOJohnston.com, and at my blog, www.KillerHobbies.blogspot.com.

Linda O. Johnston

A special, but belated, welcome to the family to Tara, who married our older son, Eric, in September 2008. Love to you both. May you both be as happy together as Fred and I have been over the years. That's not to say you won't face hurdles, but it's worth leaping over them together! And lots of love also to our younger son, Keith.

Chapter 1

The Angeles Beach SWAT team leader held up his gloved hand to signal the guys to get ready.

Oh, yeah, Officer Trevor Owens was ready. Poised to rush into the auto parts warehouse, he aimed his modified AK-47 assault rifle toward the building. All set for this potential high-risk entry.

Just give the word.

This would be one hell of a dynamic infiltration. His team would shoot to disable. But if they had to kill, they would.

This suspect had gotten away with sexual assault

and murder at least once, probably more. It wouldn't happen again. No matter what happened here today, Trevor would see to it that this guy couldn't harm another innocent civilian.

The team leader, Wesley Danver, signaled the breach man, who immediately busted the door open with a ram. "Angeles Beach P.D.," Wes yelled. "Arrest warrant for Jerome Marinaro."

The five officers, all clad in protective gear, barged in, weapons ready. Even in the dimness, Trevor could see the place was a mess. Stacks of pallets of different heights formed uneven rows on the concrete floor— all filled with boxes and metal car parts and stuff Trevor wasn't about to figure out now. He sighted along his weapon, aimed and let up as no one appeared. Then he rushed forward, pivoted and did it again.

"Go! Go! Marinaro? Where the hell is he?" Shouts reverberated through the place—Trevor's among them—amplified by the electronic equipment in his headgear. The warehouse reeked of gasoline, motor oil and mustiness, and he inhaled it all as the adrenaline rush made him breathe hard.

Where was their target? The tip that had sent them tearing over here had seemed reliable.

The suspect could be hiding behind one of those damned uneven piles or even on top of one. A cornered animal with no regard for human life, preparing to fight back.

Unless he wasn't here. The tip could've been wrong. Or he could have heard or seen them, fled already. Or—

"There he is!" came a shout from Trevor's right.

"Drop your weapon," yelled another voice. "Do it."

Trevor saw the figure off to his side, aiming something in their direction. It fired, the explosion loud in this vast warehouse.

In front of him, Wes went down.

"You SOB," hollered Trevor as he aimed his assault rifle. He fired as he heard more reports from the suspect's weapon.

Suddenly he felt pain. Excruciating pain—in his neck, just above his protective vest.

Then nothing.

Outside the warehouse, Officer Skye Rydell heard the gunshots, which sounded like a battery of AK-47s—loud, hollow, powerful. Damn! Skye knew that the SWAT team—Special Weapons And Tactics—prided itself on resolving situations peacefully. Most of the time. But apparently not today.

"Easy, Bella," Skye said. She was so attuned to her K-9 partner's whine that she could hear it despite all other noise. She glanced down. The nearly black Belgian Malinois sat obediently at her side on the pavement, obviously straining to move.

As suddenly as the noise had erupted, silence fell—except for the sound of choppers overhead.

Skye had been waiting across the street with her fellow officers who were also clad in the navy blue Angeles Beach P.D. uniform. Black-and-white patrol cars blocked the street and other non-SWAT officers watched.

The suspect had allegedly assaulted a female victim earlier that day in a location down the street from here, then shot and killed her. When confronted, he threatened half a dozen other civilians and ran into this warehouse—entirely out of control. That was why the SWAT team had been ordered to enter first.

But now weapons had been fired. No matter who had fired first, the likelihood was that the suspect was down, and since Bella was trained primarily as a felony suspect search dog, there was probably nothing for Skye and her to do.

At least, there was no need for Skye's official services. And under these circumstances, no use for her unofficial ones, either, unless...

"Officer down, officer down!" came the shout,

first from the radio on her Sam Browne utility belt and then from everywhere.

She felt Bella tremble beneath her hand. "Okay, girl," she whispered. They had to go. Now. If anyone asked questions, they were simply doing their duty, making sure the suspect hadn't escaped.

With one hand on the Glock holstered at her hip, Skye dashed across the street, holding Bella's lead as the dog loped beside her. Other officers preceded them inside the warehouse. The place was as dim as twilight, with only faint illumination from the fixtures high above, probably just the security lights. No one had turned on anything brighter. No need. SWAT equipment would allow them to see in the dark if necessary.

The place reverberated with additional shouts from fellow officers. The adrenaline rush triggered at the moment Skye had heard the shots was suddenly overshadowed by sorrow and sympathy and anger.

Officer down.

How bad were the wounds?

Was anyone dying? Dead?

Smells filled the air and her head. The bitter smokiness of spent ammunition. Oil or something similar. Blood. She could only imagine what the odors were doing to her scent-sensitive partner. Reaching down, she stroked Bella's head.

Turning a corner around a stack of pallets, she saw two other officers near an inert body on the floor. One was trying to stanch the flow of blood with the wounded man's own shirt. The other had his weapon drawn in case the suspect was nearby. Damn! She didn't want, didn't need an audience.

"Over there!" she exclaimed, pointing back to the way she had come. "I'll take over." She muscled them away, and both officers seemed grateful to leave and go after the suspect.

"Stay back, Bella," she told her partner.

She dropped to her knees and tugged off the standard-issue cap with the badge on the front. Her hair remained away from her face, held back by a clip at her nape.

It was Danver. Though she didn't know the SWAT officer well, she recognized him. His face was pasty and pinched, his eyes closed.

While pressing his shirt against the wound, Skye took Danver's wrist and checked his pulse. Faint. She held on to him, absorbing his condition.

Very near death. Too near for Skye to save him.

Abruptly, a pounding began in Skye's brain, a familiar rhythm that she had heard many times before. A chant of female voices—

It was time.

Danver's closed eyes opened wide. He lifted the arm closest to Skye and motioned vaguely toward her.

She took his hand to comfort him—and to read him, to sense who he was, what he had done in his life and whether she could do anything to help him.

As she pressed the wounded man's hand between both of hers, the chill of his flesh sent what felt like ice shards into her bloodstream. But, yes, her initial impulse was clearly correct. It was time. And she could, would, assist him.

Be strong, Officer Danver. All will be well.

Skye nodded slightly as she listened to the familiar voices chanting inside her head—intoned in the tongue of her ancestors, words understood by insight and not by translation.

She felt Danver squeeze her fingers and looked down at him again. His eyes were open but glazing over. He appeared frightened. Angry, maybe.

"It'll be all right," she whispered. "You'll see. Much better than this," she said as his body spasmed in obvious agony and he cried out. She squeezed back, willing him free of pain. His hand went slack as his eyes dulled, and Skye knew he was gone.

She closed her eyes without letting go of him. A new but familiar rhythm pulsed through her. Colors shifted before her and coagulated into a long, barely arched rainbow across the horizon of the vision inside her head. Two black silhouettes moved across it. Skye realized she'd been projected into the vision and was now walking on the shifting surface beside the shadowy wraith that had been the dying man. He strode with determination. He smiled at her. Now he understood.

The image lasted only moments before she crossed back. Alone.

She forced her eyes open, gently let go of Danver's hand and eased his eyelids down over his unseeing eyes. Dead. At peace. As always, she was proud that she could help. She was also filled with sorrow, as she was each time she had to help someone die.

She blinked her tears away, inhaled sharply and forced herself to breathe naturally. She wanted only to curl up and sleep, but she fought it off because Danver was not the only officer down.

She stood, shoving her cap into her belt. Bella brushed against her. "I'm okay, girl," she said to her partner.

EMTs had arrived and were surrounded by cops for protection. A couple of them pushed past her to see what they could do for Danver. They would soon discover their attempts to resuscitate him would be in vain.

Others were already working frantically on the other guy. Skye maneuvered around them with Bella right beside her and stood looking over the shoulder of a crouching EMT. This victim was dressed in a SWAT uniform, but most of his gear had been stripped away, laying bare his torn neck and bloody chest.

The pounding rhythm—the chanting, the keening—started once more inside Skye's mind.

There was another decision to make. Was he yet another fallen hero she needed to help to the other side?

The cop was apparently breathing…barely. Fortunately, they'd already taken the first steps to stop the bleeding and were now busy setting up their medical equipment. Not watching her.

She took the man's hand and stared at his face. *Owens.* She recognized him, too. Not that they'd often gotten within twenty feet of each other. In Angeles Beach, the SWAT team trained alone.

His features were strong and masculine—so appealing that she had an urge to stroke his slack cheek. *Get real, Rydell.* She had work to do here. Fast.

As she continued to grasp Owens's limp hand, a sensation pulsed through her, startling her. There was something this officer had left to accomplish—needed to accomplish.

She had felt it in the other injured people whose

lives she had determined to save. It was an important factor in her split-second decisions.

Those she had saved had never been so far gone. But, with this man, there was something utterly critical yet to come in his future. That was what she felt. What she *knew*. And there was more. Something disquieting. Something important to her? A bond of some kind between them?

She sensed some intense emotions inside his mind as well as a determination to survive.

"You've got to move, Officer," an EMT shouted. She ignored him for an instant.

This cop could not die. She would not permit it even though she felt his spirit approach the bridge where Danver had crossed.

You will live. It is not yet your time. Open your eyes. The unspoken voice issuing commands was hers, and it was inundating him with a life force that flowed intentionally, excruciatingly, from her.

Officer Owens groaned and his eyes opened. They were dark, the deep brown of polished mahogany, and stared straight into Skye's.

"Holy shit," said one of the EMTs. "I thought this guy'd had it. But look at those vitals. Atta way, sir!"

They'd hooked Owens up to some monitors. Apparently whatever showed there looked promising.

Yes, Skye thought as she stood up and got out of the way. *You will live.*

That didn't make up for helping the other officer to die, but it lessened her pain, a little.

Although utterly exhausted, she managed to smile down at Owens, soothingly and encouragingly.

And when he gazed faintly back at her while lying there with blood covering his badly injured body, a sensation she could not identify rolled through Skye. Recognition? Pleasure? Satisfaction? Anticipation?

All of them?

Time to get out of there. Bella and she had work to do, and it didn't involve daydreaming.

And yet, she couldn't help watching as Owens's eyes closed again. Slowly. Peacefully.

He *was* going to live.

Skye hoped that whatever she'd sensed he'd needed to do was worth it and that he would in fact accomplish it.

She nearly stumbled over her own shuffling feet as she took Bella's collar and made her way out of the warehouse.

In the chaos outside, she was handed a shirt by another officer. "Suspect's still at large. Got this from his automobile—ran his plate. See if Bella can find this bastard."

Skye led Bella back inside to where officers who'd witnessed the shooting said the suspect had stood to shoot the two downed men. She held the shirt out, and Bella sniffed it.

She immediately picked up the scent. Skye followed—until Bella lost track of it in the parking lot outside. She couldn't pick it up again.

The suspect must have stolen a different vehicle. He was gone.

Chapter 2

"That's why you feel so tired," said Hayley Sigurd. The willowy ice-blonde who'd been Skye's friend since childhood smiled sympathetically. Although she'd kept her voice low, it was unnecessary. Bernardo's at the Beach wasn't only the favorite dinner hangout of Skye's group of transplanted Minnesotans, it was also Angeles Beach's most popular restaurant, and the boisterous crowd around their table of four was noisy enough that no one could be eavesdropping.

"Yeah," agreed Kara Woods, at Skye's left. "Helping

the first guy pass over was draining all by itself. And if that second guy was as gone as you say…" Kara was the most curvaceous of them. Her straight black hair belied her mother's Nordic ancestry, but her dad's side of family was Native American, and her strikingly sharp features had come from him…just as her powers, like Skye's and Hayley's, had come from her mom's side of the family.

"Of course he was." Ron Gollar jutted his broad, smooth chin out belligerently as if expecting the women to contradict him…as usual. Like the others, Skye sometimes enjoyed giving Ron a hard time for fun, but not today, when she felt utterly serious and drained.

Although Ron was also twenty-seven, he was like Skye's little brother. He'd been in the marines for a while and now was a rookie ABPD cop. He had been at the warehouse, but not close enough to the victims to see how far gone they were. At the moment, he was just being supportive of Skye, which made her want to hug him.

Skye sipped her peach margarita, feeling the sweet alcohol drink slip through her, relaxing her even more. She stared out at the golden sky. The sun was just setting over the Pacific, a beautiful, peaceful twilight that also helped to mellow her mood. As exhausted as she'd felt since her work at the crime scene that afternoon, she'd also been edgy. Worried. Had she made the right choices this time?

And what was that odd sensation she had felt about the second victim, Owens? Since she'd left his side, she'd ached to see him again—to assure herself he really would be all right, to try to understand his unassailable need to survive, and why she had felt so compelled to save his life.

"It's the first time I ever took on two victims at the same time," she said to her friends. "How do you two handle it?"

Kara was an emergency medical technician. She faced multiple casualties nearly every day. And Hayley, who was on her way toward becoming a trauma surgeon, did as well. As a male, Ron did not share their unique abilities and never had to engage in the life-and-death decisions that Skye shared with her female friends. Friends whose mothers, like hers, were all descended from Valkyries.

The waitress came to the table balancing delectable-looking salads containing greens with nuts and fruit, smothered in raspberry vinaigrette. "Here you are," she said. "The rest of your food will be up shortly."

Skye used her fork to play with a piece of arugula. The others dug in right away, though, even Ron.

"You'll get used to it, honey," Kara eventually said. Her piercing, hazel eyes had gone as sympathetic as Hayley's blue ones. "It is exhausting, though. Drains our own life force. I've even managed to bring back a couple of guys from a motorcycle accident at the exact same time—although neither was as far gone as the officer you described."

"Doesn't it help when you can also use regular life-saving medical stuff, too?" Ron took a piece of bread from a basket. He'd curved his broad shoulders beneath his white T-shirt as if waiting to be criticized. "You two have it easier than a cop like Skye, don't you?"

"How would you know, twerp?" Hayley asked good-naturedly. Then she frowned, creating lines on her high forehead that the wispy bangs of her pale hair didn't quite conceal. "But you're right, Ron. Kara and I always use whatever resources we can and Skye has her Bella, who helps her find the bad guys. But we're all stuck with making tough decisions about which people should live and which should die."

All were silent for a moment, and Skye felt the weight of what Hayley had said.

They could have stayed in the familiar environment where their families had resided for over a century. There, in a small Minnesota town, their mothers and their mothers' mothers, only had to use their special life-preserving powers on rare occasions when those who were young and healthy and not ready to head toward the afterlife suffered accidents or other life-threatening situations and needed to be brought back from the brink. No need for the split-second decisions that had to be made in other circumstances. Most of the time, their mothers merely held the hands of the elderly and infirm—those clearly at the crossroads between life and death—easing them to the other side.

Over the years, a few with their powers had left the area, intending to partake in a broader mission, but it hadn't been the majority.

Until now. Skye's generation was different. Many chose to leave so they could use their powers to reach out in secret and help people in other communities whose females did not share their powers.

Skye and her three closest friends had often talked about moving to where trauma was an everyday occurrence, to maximize the number of lives they saved and those whose ends they eased. Ron could not actively participate, but he'd made it clear he wanted to join them and help however he could.

Eventually, they'd settled on Angeles Beach. Near L.A. and growing almost as fast, it had more than its share of violence. And by the time they'd arrived, they each had decided on what path to take to achieve their goals.

Skye had already trained in law enforcement at home and was a K-9 cop. With a caring, nonhuman partner, she could achieve what she needed to with as much secrecy as possible.

She had already assisted quite a few people to the other side and had brought others back. But not fellow cops. And not anyone like Owens.

"You okay, Skye?" Hayley reached her slender hand over and patted Skye's arm. "If you're too tired to eat, we'll get our dinners to go and I'll drive you home."

"No way!" Skye yanked her thoughts back to where they belonged. "I'm fine," she said. "Hey, there's our food."

The waitress was back with their mostly seafood entrées, and Skye joined in with the good-natured banter and sharing of bites that followed.

But in the back of her mind, she wondered about the man whose life she had snatched from certain death.

What was it about SWAT Officer Trevor Owens that now intrigued her?

Trevor felt as if he'd been run over by one of the Robotic Offensive Bomb vehicles used by the ABPD's bomb squad.

He lay still and exhausted in his hospital bed, knowing it was only the drugs being sucked into his bloodstream via the IV needle in his arm that kept him from hurting like hell.

The room was tiny, but it was all his. There was no one to fight him for control over the TV mounted overhead, but he didn't even have enough strength to push a button on the remote. All he could do was wonder how—and why—he'd survived.

He'd thought he was dying. Dead. Killed in the line of duty, protecting the public from a suspect who'd taken down yet another civilian victim and now a cop, too. Danver, damn it! His team leader didn't deserve that.

Trevor had always figured that would be how he'd go. On his own time, though. Up against a guilty suspect who'd gotten away with murder before Trevor was on him. A suspect about to be stopped from doing it again, even if Trevor had to die to take him down.

But Trevor hadn't had a chance to do things his way. He'd had to play by the book this time, and what had it gotten him?

Shot in the neck. The kind of wound that's usually fatal. But he hadn't died. Instead, he'd heard someone telling him to get his ass in gear and get back to the world of the living.

Then he'd opened his eyes to find that hot blond female K-9 officer staring at him. It seemed as if she was the one hollering in his head to wake up.

Rydell was her name. She was relatively new to the force—not that his guys fraternized much with the rest of the department. He'd met her, seen her around, definitely noticed her. But had he ever talked to her?

Not that he remembered. But—

The phone rang. It was on a little table right beside him, and it took all his concentration to swivel and pick up the receiver. "Yeah?"

"Owens, that you?" It was Greg Blanding, a fellow SWAT officer and Trevor's closest bud on the force.

"What do you want? You were here only a few minutes ago."

"Try a few hours ago. And I'm just about to go into the captain's debriefing about your big show yesterday."

"Say hi to them all for me."

"Yeah. Will do." Blanding sounded as if he was getting misty-eyed. Hell.

"Any word on Marinaro?" Trevor asked gruffly.

"No, but I'll let you know if I hear of anything at the meeting."

"Good." He paused. "We gotta get that SOB."

"Yeah." Blanding's tone was icy now. "Gotta run. I'll call again later. You okay?"

"Sure, if feeling like my neck's been run over by an R.O.B. vehicle is okay."

Blanding laughed. "Got it. Talk to you soon."

"Hey, do me a favor."

"What's that?"

"That K-9 officer, Rydell? If she's at the meeting, tell her I need to talk to her. Right away."

"Why?"

Damned if he knew. But it felt urgent. Like his life depended on it.

He had to give Blanding some explanation. "She must be my lucky charm. I opened my eyes after I was shot, and what did I see? Her face."

"Not a bad face, either," Blanding said, sounding as if he was getting all worked up just thinking about Rydell.

"Go screw yourself, Blanding. And her, too." Now, why the hell had he said that? It only made him wild to think his friend might even consider getting it on with that gorgeous, sexy woman whom he now had one hell of an urge to talk to.

"I'll leave that to you, sir," Blanding said with a laugh as he hung up.

Blanding's remark peeved Trevor even more, but it gave him a sudden surge of strength, which made it possible for him to pick up the remote and push the button to turn on the TV news.

"Easy," Skye whispered to Bella, whose head kept turning as more people entered the roll call room. Captain Boyd Franks had called a late-afternoon debriefing after yesterday's warehouse situation. Everyone who'd been on duty yesterday was to attend, except for those patrolling beats right now.

Skye, still tired but functioning, sat uncomfortably on a chair at the end of a row. She had chosen a place in the middle of the room, which was now filled with the pulsing hum of dozens of conversations.

Ron slipped in beside her and lifted his hand in greeting to a couple of the guys.

It looked like her pal was fitting in well—maybe even better than she was even though she'd been in Angeles Beach for about eight months. Skye hadn't spent a lot of time getting to know her fellow cops. Getting too chummy with them might make it harder to do what she had to, when she had to do it.

Bella whined, and Ron gave her a rough pat. "How you doin', girl?"

Skye smiled. "Her or me?"

"Both."

As the rush of people into the room slowed, Captain Franks took his place at the wooden dais at the front. Skye guessed he was nearing retirement age, with silver hair adorning a long face whose dourness and deep wrinkles suggested he'd experienced plenty of bad stuff in his time with the department. He wore a lot of stripes along the arm of his blue uniform, each signifying five years of service.

"Listen up," he bellowed to get everyone's attention. The buzzing stopped abruptly. "Thanks. We're here to go over the events at that auto parts warehouse yesterday."

"How's Owens?" shouted someone near the front of the room.

Skye's heart started to race.

"Wanna give us an update, Blanding?" Franks called, looking into the sea of uniforms seated in front of him.

"I visited him at the hospital, just talked to him, too. The guy's one tough bird. Most of the bullets hit his vest, but one got him above it, in the neck. Don't know how, but it managed not to do a whole lot of damage. He'll be sore for a while, but he'll be okay."

A cheer erupted throughout the room, and Skye joined in. She was as pleased as anyone that Owens would survive. Maybe more than most. She knew exactly how the bullet failed to do permanent damage, but she wasn't about to mention it.

"Let's not forget about Danver," Captain Franks said, pouring icy water onto their brief celebration. A low, grief-filled rumble ensued.

"When's the funeral?" called someone.

"Next week. We need enough time to make sure everyone who wants to get here can make it." The captain's voice rasped now, and Skye again felt tears rush to her eyes.

She'd done what she had to and made dying at least a little easier for Danver.

But it still hurt, and she hardly even knew him.

"Anyone spotted Marinaro?" someone else shouted. The rumble turned into a roar of fury.

"Not yet," the captain admitted. He looked as enraged as everyone else in the crowded room. "But we'll get him."

Shouts of agreement echoed off the walls.

For a short while, the captain went over what was being done to track the suspect. A special team was being formed to follow up on any leads—assuming some came in.

The person who'd called in with the initial tip that had led them to the warehouse had apparently disappeared. It wasn't clear whether she'd fled in fear…or whether Marinaro had found her first.

Soon, the meeting adjourned, and rows of uniformed officers filed out, rumbling and swatting each other on the arms, obviously glad to be alive despite their anger about their fallen comrade.

"You on duty this evening?" Ron asked as they waited for the others in their row to leave. "I am— I'm patrolling downtown."

"No, soon as I finish my report Bella and I are through for the day." She needed to rest. This meeting had made Skye feel…well, helpless—as if she'd initiated something important, yet left it undone.

It wasn't up to Bella and her to locate Marinaro now, yet she itched to find the suspect and bring him down.

"You okay, Skye?" Ron asked.

"Just fine," she said. "I was only thinking of what the captain said, and wondering how, with all of us around like that, Marinaro was able to get away."

"You're not the only one," Ron said, straightening in his uniform.

They'd reached the end of their row. Ron edged out first, but as Skye and Bella started to leave, their way was suddenly blocked.

SWAT Officer Greg Blanding stood there, his shaved head emphasizing the breadth of his slightly misshapen nose. "Skye, hope you don't mind, but I have a special request for you."

And when he told her what it was, she worked hard to maintain a straight face and nonchalant air despite the inappropriate cartwheels her insides had started to turn.

"Sure," she said. "I'm just happy Officer Owens survived. And I'd be glad to visit him in the hospital."

Chapter 3

"Want me to come with you, Skye?" Ron asked as they walked out of the roll call room door with Bella.

"Hey, Gollar, joining us for dinner?" one of the other guys called, punching his shoulder good-naturedly. "Your turn to buy."

"Yeah, yeah. Like you need it." Ron grinned at the taller and rounder cop.

The other guy was also smiling. "I'll let you try to beat me up one of these days." He went on ahead.

"I'll be fine on my own," Skye told Ron. "It looks like you have things to do."

"If you're sure…"

"Enjoy your dinner."

"Right. And you enjoy your handiwork." Ron looked a little wistful. He was a good guy, with a deep sense of right and wrong. Too bad he had to save lives the ordinary way.

Skye led Bella back toward the area in the station that contained their cubicle. She didn't have the time, or the inclination, to break for a meal. She was thinking too much about her impending visit to Trevor Owens's hospital room.

But she couldn't go immediately, and not just because she had to finish the report detailing her perspective on what happened yesterday. She had research to do. She couldn't exactly ask Owens what he was thinking when she brought him back from the dead or what made him so determined to survive. But she could arm herself with at least a little knowledge before going to see him.

"Come on, Bella." She led her companion out to the parklike fenced-in training area. The weather was Southern California perfect. The sun was shining, and it smelled…well, green and a little salty from the nearby Pacific.

She let Bella run for a few minutes but she stayed still, conserving her energy. They were soon joined by three more members of the ABPD K-9 unit, guys with young, eager German shepherds who engaged Bella in roughhousing while Skye and her fellow humans cheered them on.

"You were at that warehouse yesterday." Ken Vesco was a by-the-book cop, an African-American who was friendly with Skye despite chiding her now and then about not treating Bella enough like a dog. "I wish to hell they'd called me back on duty, but Bandit and I had already worked ten hours."

"I doubt there was more you or any of the other guys could have done," Skye said. She'd been the only K-9 handler there at the time. "Bella picked up the scent in the warehouse, but by the time she followed it outside to the parking lot the suspect was already gone."

"The bastard shot two cops," Curt Tritt said through uneven, gritted teeth. His dog was Storm.

"I want to be in on it when there's something else to go on," tall, thin Manny Igoa added. "Rusty and I'll help bring him down."

"Bella and me, too." Sure, Skye had taken on responsibilities in law enforcement for reasons far different from most of her compatriots', but she always wanted to do a good job with her regular duties—not to mention those that her fellow officers would consider quite irregular.

The others were still playing when she called Bella to go inside. She led her dog into the bull pen of cubicles shared by the K-9 team—a bunch of desks and file cabinets roughly organized in one moderate-sized room. She sat at her desk, told Bella "down" and booted up her computer.

As soon as she'd filled out her report on yesterday's warehouse incident, she opened the nonconfidential part of the ABPD employee files and looked up Trevor Owens.

And got a jolt. The guy had been with the department for nearly seven years. During that time he'd been in four officer-involved shootings besides yesterday's. In all the others, the suspect had also apparently fired first, and Owens returned fire in self-defense. Each time but this one, the suspect had died.

The Force Investigation Division had cleared Owens of any wrongdoing. That's all that was listed there—no specifics regarding any event or its review. The more detailed reports remained confidential, and although Skye might have been able to access them, she wasn't officially entitled to. Plus, if she opened them, it might raise a red flag. She couldn't do that. Her survival here depended on her remaining low-key, under the radar.

She soon left for the day with Bella and with more questions raised than answered.

After Skye showered and changed into comfortable jeans and a blue denim shirt, she walked and fed Bella. Then, leaving Bella at home, Skye drove her own car to the Angeles Beach Medical Center.

She asked at the information desk for the room number. After exiting the elevator on the correct floor and walking to his room, she paused. What the hell was she doing there?

Accepting an invitation from a downed officer, she reminded herself. Plus…satisfying her curiosity, if only a little.

Still, she hesitated at the door. Then she rapped and walked in.

The room's sole occupant was sitting up in bed. "Hello, Officer Owens," she said. "I'm Skye Rydell. I was told you wanted to see me."

"Come in." His voice was hoarse but wasn't weak or pained the way someone who'd recently been so near death might be expected to sound. That didn't surprise Skye.

His bed was raised, supporting his back as he sat straight up. He wore the kind of faded green cotton hospital wrap that made most people look ill. But despite the slight pastiness to his face, he looked healthy and tan. His sleeves were pushed up to his wide shoulders, framing impressive biceps.

As she looked at him, those brown eyes she recognized, deep and steady, met hers. A little embarrassed to be caught assessing him, she smiled uncomfortably. "You look like you're recuperating okay," she said. "How do you feel?"

"Like shit." His voice cleared as if he'd intentionally thrust away its former hoarseness. "But a whole lot better than when they brought me in. I've seen you around, you know, but I almost didn't recognize you without your dog."

That evoked a genuine smile from her. "And I almost didn't recognize you without your assault rifle."

His laugh, deep and sexy, filled the room. "Have a seat." He motioned to a chair, and she complied.

"So…why am I here?" She studied the way the guy's prominent cheekbones underscored the eyes that so defined his face. The artificial light radiating from a bar above the bed's headboard revealed a hint of auburn in his sable-brown hair. Beard stubble shadowed his taut cheeks and emphasized a cleft in his strong chin. Definitely one good-looking cop, especially this close up.

"I was told you were there when I was wounded, weren't you?"

"Outside," she replied. "We came into the ware-house—Bella and I—when you were already down."

"Yeah, after Danver was hit." He sounded offended, as if the death was a personal affront. There was a bleakness in his eyes and the set of his mouth that stirred Skye.

She couldn't exactly tell him she'd communicated with his fellow SWAT officer, helped him peacefully to the other side. "It was really terrible," she confirmed. "But at least you'll be okay."

"But the bastard who did this got away."

That was obviously on a lot of cops' minds.

"He won't get away with it," she said with certainty.

"Yeah." Trevor's grim expression suggested he would see to it himself.

Was he going to get caught up in another officer-involved shooting? Was the goal she'd sensed in him as he lay dying to right this wrong by committing a wrong himself?

She shuddered. Maybe she had made a mistake after all. Her intent, as always, was to help those who needed—and deserved—it. Was this police officer a loose cannon who would kill a suspect first and ask questions later? But he had been cleared of wrongdoing in those past shootings. There was no reason to think he would kill anyone, even Marinaro.

Even so, she had a sudden urge to leave, to never see him again.

Won't happen, taunted a perverse voice inside her. They were both part of the ABPD. They'd see each other around.

Well…okay. Good, in fact. No matter what, she was intrigued by him—wanted to understand his side of those shootings and why she had such a strong sense of connection when she saved him.

"Did you say anything to me then?" he asked. "I mean, when you saw me on the floor. I can't remember a whole lot that happened then, but I remember seeing you, and I thought I heard you say something."

"I don't think so." It wasn't a lie. She hadn't said anything…aloud. And only *she* heard her internal voices.

At least no one she had ever saved in the past had mentioned them. But, then again, she'd hardly been able to ask any of them—any more than she could ask Officer Trevor Owens.

There are other things you could learn from him, that same internal voice taunted. Like his apparent intense desire to get the bad guy?

Or just *desire.*

She felt herself flush from uneasiness…and

sexual attraction. And as their eyes caught again, there was more that made her uncomfortably warm.

No way could Trevor Owens know that she had restored him to life…or could he?

Trevor knew for sure now that he was still alive.

Her slim, coplike yet gracefully curvy form and her intoxicating scent made him ache. He wanted this woman.

Yeah, as if your body could follow through right now.

She was interested, too. He could tell from the look on her face. But Trevor knew Officer Skye Rydell was lying about something.

What? And why?

He studied her.

He liked seeing her in civilian clothes and with loose hair. He wondered what women called that shade of blond—or those shades. It was streaked— some strands were almost white, though most were several shades darker. She usually wore it pulled back and fastened behind her neck as required by the department. With it loose, she looked even more female.

Being so close to her let him get a good look at her gorgeous face—smooth, with a perfectly shaped if slightly long nose and lips that, even without lipstick, were pink and full and suggested slow, hot kisses at midnight on a deserted local beach.

The pale denim blue of her shirt deepened the blue of her eyes. Those eyes... One of the few things he remembered from when he was lying on the floor was looking up into those intense eyes and feeling as if they were lifting him back to life.

But it wasn't only the way she'd looked at him that he remembered.

When he was barely conscious, he had the odd sensation that he shared something with her. Something vital. Hallucinations by a guy close to death? Sure. What else could it be?

"You're sure you didn't say anything?" he finally asked again.

Something different—perhaps embarrassment?—passed across her face.

She might be a liar, but she wasn't a very good one.

But why lie about something so trivial?

"You didn't look very well, so I might have murmured some good wishes or a prayer or something like that."

Something like that. But what?

"Well, anyway, I asked Greg Blanding to call you for me. I figured I'd thank you."

For what? Hell, he didn't know. If things had gone as he'd assumed at the time, he wouldn't have seen this woman, or anyone else, ever again.

"I can't imagine why, but you're welcome."

"They say I won't be out of here for a few days."

"I'm sure they want to make certain you're all right," she said. "Anyway, I don't want to tire you out." She rose.

He wanted her to stay. "I'm fine. Honest. If you sit back down, I'll tell you my life story."

She laughed. "If I sit back down, I'll tell you *my* life story, and then you'll be so bored you'll sleep till they let you out of here."

"I'll take that chance."

"No, really, I have to go. Bella's waiting at home."

"Your dog? She's great."

"Yes, she is."

"Will you come see me again?" Damn. He sounded like a begging wuss who'd never seen a pretty woman before. "I mean, I'd like your view of what happened. How that SOB got away with all of us there."

"I imagine you'll get a better perspective from your fellow SWAT team members," she said, appearing puzzled.

"Yeah, but I figured a K-9 officer's ideas would be interesting."

"Well… I'm sure I'll see you around once you're back on active duty."

She'd reached the door and was almost out. Almost gone. But he knew there was something more, something she could—should—tell him that was critical to what had happened to him.

He'd thought he was dead. He survived. She wouldn't be able to tell him more about it…would she?

"I'll see you before then," he called after her. "You can count on it."

Chapter 4

Three days had passed since the incident.

Skye was sitting in her cubicle with Bella before starting their assignments for the day and thinking about how frayed everyone's nerves remained—especially since there had been no breakthrough in their hunt for the suspect, Marinaro.

On top of that, the Force Investigation Division was not inclined to let much time elapse between the officer-involved shootings and their incisive debriefings that also played havoc with everyone's psyches.

Her interview was in five minutes.

Relax, she ordered herself. It wouldn't be too bad. The FID was speaking with all members of the ABPD who'd been deployed to the site that day. Since they wanted as complete a story as possible, the FID representatives had to talk to everyone, even those who couldn't contribute much to the description of what had happened.

They would assume that included her, so how detailed could they be? It wasn't as if they had any inkling about her real role that day in the aftermath of the officer-involved shootings.

"Come on, Bella," she told her partner, who was alert, as always, to her every move. "I'll let you hang out with the other dogs while I'm busy."

Tritt and Vesco were outside conducting an informal training session with their K-9 partners Storm and Bandit. They agreed to include Bella in their lesson, which gave Skye a little relief as she trudged back inside the station. She took the stairs to the top floor, the sixth, where the brass had their offices.

One small conference room had been commandeered by the FID for their interviews. In the hallway, Skye straightened her uniform and touched the back of her head where her hair was pulled into its usual clip. Then she knocked on the wood frame of the door that surrounded panels of frosted glass.

"Come in," called a voice from inside.

She opened the door and hesitated. Three people sat around the table: Captain Boyd Franks, Lieutenant Theresa Agnew—who, though only in her mid-forties, was the head of the FID—and civilian member John Correy. Skye had met them all before—and had hoped never to face them in an official inquiry.

Captain Franks waved her to a hard wooden chair at the head of the polished table and introduced her to the others. "Thanks for joining us," he finished.

As if she had a choice.

"As you know," Lieutenant Agnew said in a crisp, formal tone, "it's our responsibility to look into all officer-involved shootings and make certain they were handled appropriately."

Skye nodded and wondered if any of these people had participated in the hearings related to the previous shootings Trevor Owens had been involved in. But what did she care? She had no reason to assume the man was too quick on the trigger. This time he apparently hadn't even gotten off a single shot before he was hit.

Her mind focused briefly on her first glimpse of him on the floor. Bleeding. Dying… All but dead.

She must have made a face, since John Correy
said, "We know it was an unpleasant situation, and
that you were not in the thick of it, so this meeting
is only a formality. We'd like you to tell us where you
were stationed when the shots were fired and what
you did next."

"Of course." Skye went through the explanation, mostly for Correy's benefit, of her role as a
K-9 cop whose partner was trained primarily to
search for suspects at a crime scene. "My dog,
Bella, and I were waiting outside in case we were
needed. That's when I heard the shots and went in,
hoping to help apprehend the suspect should he
have gotten away."

"Which he did," Lieutenant Agnew said dryly.
"Did you and your dog search for him?"

"Yes. Bella got the scent from a shirt one of the
officers took from the suspect's car and tracked him
to where another vehicle may have been parked. I
concluded he drove away, perhaps in a stolen vehicle."

"And that was your only involvement," Captain
Franks prompted, not making it a question.

"Yes, sir." The lie came easily. Skye had been
doing everything necessary to protect her secret. If
she told the truth, no one would believe her anyway.
She would lose her job. Maybe even land in some

kind of touchy-feely, and utterly unnecessary, psychological counseling.

"But why did you come inside in the first place, Officer Rydell?" John Correy asked coldly. "Were you given orders to enter?"

"Not expressly, sir." She felt on edge. How should she handle this? "I heard someone yell 'Officer down' and ran in to see if I could help. But the EMTs arrived soon, so that was that."

"You were on the floor beside both our injured officers," Lieutenant Agnew said.

No surprise that her presence had been noticed. She'd already thought through what to say, just as she had other times she'd used her abilities. Only, this situation was different from the rest. The people she helped were fellow cops. She would keep it short and simple. "Yes, ma'am," she said softly. "I…I just felt so awful I acted on instinct. I wanted so badly to help, but of course I couldn't."

"Of course," Captain Franks said. "I think that's all, Officer Rydell. Thank you."

Thank you, Captain. She didn't wait to see if the others would contradict him. She rose, nodded respectfully and hurried from the room.

Skye stood outside the door after shutting it behind her. She closed her eyes briefly, leaned against the wall to catch her breath, then opened them again.

She thought it had gone okay, but how could she really know?

Perhaps she had overstepped what appeared to be her boundaries as a K-9 cop. She had apparently acted unprofessionally by letting her feelings rule and approaching the downed officers. But surely the worst that would happen was a reprimand, rather than termination from the job…right?

At least she had not given away her real reason for getting so close….

Okay, time to get out of here. She squared her shoulders and headed toward the elevator. Her legs felt too wobbly to chance the stairs.

Her mind focused again on her real reason for getting so close, at least to the second downed officer. How was Trevor Owens doing now? She pushed the elevator button and waited only a few seconds before the light went on to signal a car had arrived.

The door opened…and Skye found herself looking right into the alert—and quizzical—eyes of Officer Trevor Owens.

Trevor blinked, then allowed the corners of his mouth to turn up into a slow smile. "Hello, Skye."

Damn, it was good to see her again, especially now that his body was closer to being healed and well enough to react to her sexiness.

He got off the elevator and expected her to enter the car, but she didn't. Instead, she stood there as the door closed behind him. "What are you doing here?" she asked. Her uniform was crisp and professional, but though her blond hair was pulled away from her face, she managed to appear attractively disheveled.

Maybe it was the exhaustion and wariness in her brilliant blue eyes, or the way a few strands of her hair had managed to escape and frame her pink cheeks.

"Unless there's something you know that I don't, I still work for the department." He widened his grin.

Her flush deepened. "I meant... Well, I'm glad you're feeling well enough to be here, but—you're not on active duty, are you?"

His smile disappeared. "Not yet."

"Are you—"

"I'm healing amazingly well. That's what they told me at the hospital before releasing me this morning."

"I'm glad." Skye's gaze met his for a long moment before she looked away. The intensity of their gaze reminded him of when he'd been down. And something about that still bothered him.

"Officer Owens," boomed Captain Franks's voice as the conference room door opened. "Come in. How are you feeling?" The captain glanced sideways at Skye, as if questioning her presence, and she reached beyond Trevor to push the elevator button several times, trying to act as if she'd just been standing there waiting impatiently for it to arrive.

"I've felt better, sir," Trevor told the commanding officer, knowing the question would be repeated over and over till he was completely healed. "But I'm doing okay."

The elevator dinged, and Trevor glanced toward Skye as she hustled into it. "See you around, Officer Rydell," he called.

She mumbled something, but he couldn't quite hear it.

Inside the conference room, Trevor hesitated briefly. Only two more FID people sat there—people who knew the score. In hearings related to other officer-involved shootings, he'd sometimes had to face as many as half a dozen examiners—but fortunately they'd always included Franks, Agnew and Correy.

This time would be a piece of cake. He had been shot. Hadn't shot back. This time, the inquiry was merely a formality.

"Good to see you looking so well, Officer Owens." Theresa stood and smiled at him.

"I heard your injuries were life threatening," Correy said as he approached and held out his hand.

"That's what I was told," Trevor agreed. "But I'll be fine."

They motioned him to sit at the head of the table, then asked questions about what had gone down in that warehouse, how the team had entered and whether everything had been done by the book.

He was glad they didn't ask how he felt and what he saw when he was down.

How could he have possibly explained the agony he had suffered, the bright light he'd seen, the compulsion to open his eyes and look into the blue, concerned depths of Skye Rydell's eyes, or the sensation that she had been calling to him, insisting that he live?

He couldn't. It seemed so ridiculous.

Soon, the questions ended. "We'll be in touch if we need anything more from you, Trevor," the captain said. "Meantime, take the time you need to heal. We're all pulling for you to get back, but not before you're ready."

"We're all glad you're okay," Theresa Agnew said again. "Any questions for us before we adjourn?"

"One," Trevor said grimly. "What's the word on Marinaro's location?"

"Unknown," Captain Franks said, "but we'll get him."

"Yeah," Trevor said. He hoped they'd get him fast. Before he could hurt anyone else—civilian or cop.

Best of all would be if Marinaro stayed at large just long enough for Trevor to apprehend him…his way.

He should have left well enough alone and gone home as he was supposed to. But Trevor poked his head into a few offices at the station, receiving the applause of coworkers who were glad to see he was alive.

He couldn't resist going over to the K-9 officers' domain, which was filled with closely spaced cubicles and hooks from which leather leashes hung. There was a slight doggy aroma and an atmosphere of readiness to run that must have been created by the dogs sitting at attention near some desks.

Trevor was glad to note that one of the dogs was the black one assigned to Skye Rydell. Seeing Trevor, she stood and wagged her tail eagerly. So did a few other dogs. The K-9 handlers did as other people in the station had done.

"Good to see you, man," said Tritt, who was near retirement and as mangy-looking as his dog.

"Glad you're okay," said Igoa, a huge grin lighting his narrow face.

But even while receiving their kudos, Trevor let his gaze remain on someone else. Skye was on the phone. She looked up, nodded cordially, but seemed in no hurry to congratulate him again on surviving.

On impulse, Trevor approached her when she hung up. "Hey, Skye." He patted Bella on her sleek head. "Wanna grab a cup of coffee with me? I'd still like your opinion on what happened at that warehouse. What you saw, and all."

"I just told the FID committee everything," she said. "I'd really rather not go over it again." She let her gaze rise just a little, but wouldn't allow herself to completely meet his eyes.

Skye had seemed a little uneasy when she'd visited him at the hospital, but now she appeared really uncomfortable.

Why? What was she hiding? Had she known the suspect? Somehow been involved?

Unlikely, but she was definitely concealing something.

Right now they had an audience of her coworkers, so he wouldn't press the point.

But he was definitely going to find out what Officer Skye Rydell wasn't telling him.

Chapter 5

It was Monday, a week after the warehouse incident, and along with everyone else in the Angeles Beach P.D., Skye was edgy. Marinaro was still at large.

Stories and questions kept appearing in the news. Tips poured in. But no lead had resulted in locating Marinaro.

The person who'd phoned in the tip that led them to the warehouse had finally been found. She worked in the warehouse and was offered witness protection until Marinaro was caught and convicted.

And talk about media frenzy: today was Officer Wesley Danver's funeral. Reporters were everywhere.

At the moment, Skye stood on a paved path along the cemetery's steep hillside that faced the Pacific below. She had arrived early with the rest of the K-9 unit, ostensibly to help keep order among the masses of people attending the interment. Members of law enforcement departments from across the country filed in to pay their respects to the officer killed in the line of duty. The parade of vehicles had begun early that morning along the city's thoroughfares and hadn't stopped, though the funeral was scheduled to begin in half an hour.

The Angeles Beach Police Department was on alert, observing attendees. Killers often came to their victims' funerals. Even cop killers.

Jerome Marinaro might be hiding in plain sight, in a uniform or suit. The best way to penetrate a good disguise would be for one of the dogs to identify him by scent.

Since Bella had been the only dog at the scene that day, she had an edge over the others.

"Lotta people," said Ken Vesco, who stood beside Skye holding his German shepherd's leash. Like Skye, he watched the crowd enter through the gates at the cemetery's entrance and spread out over the hillside.

"Sure are," Skye agreed.

A lot of living souls, but they weren't the only people Skye was thinking about. Below green, manicured grass lined with stone markers were a lot of deceased people. This was the main Angeles Beach cemetery, and it was huge. Buildings held crypts containing multiple layers of decedents' remains, often grouped in families with spaces reserved for those to follow.

Skye inhaled slowly, sadly. She was far from a stranger to death and its ultimate inevitability, but despite all her childhood training with family members and others who understood, she still felt every loss personally—even when she was unable to do more than assist a worthy, dying person to the best of the other side. Especially then.

Her decisions were critical, though. They were irrevocable and based on immediate impressions of the person at the crossroads between life and death. Often, she chose to restore life. Sometimes, she didn't.

Too bad the ancient legends were only partly true. Some form of existence lay on the other side, of course, but not exactly the exalted Valhalla of stories—or so today's Valkyrie descendants believed.

Skye's ancestresses may have chosen which valiant soldiers would live and which would cross over, but descriptions of what Valkyries in those days looked like, how the dead were treated in the halls of Valhalla and why… The variety and inconsistency of tales proved that no one who knew the truth had disclosed it to the living—or, if they had, it had not been glamorous enough to be passed down through time.

As she was growing up, Skye's family and friends often discussed the legends, but despite their important role in end-of-life decisions, no one could describe the afterlife for certain. No one who completed their crossing of the rainbow bridge, with or without assistance, ever came back to tell. But today's descendants were sure there was a pleasant plane of existence to look forward to on the other side.

Some people did not deserve to be there. A fortunate few of them had their forevers saved by being assisted across the bridge by a Valkyrie descendant who sensed something salvageable within them. The rest wound up elsewhere, the equivalent of purgatory or hell—someplace too awful to describe.

Maybe if she knew for certain, it would make her chosen path easier, give her even more hope to pass along to those she helped to die.

Skye realized that she had been craning her neck, watching for the other person she had helped that day…*really* helped.

Almost as if he had heard her, Officer Trevor Owens emerged from the crowd just below and walked slowly up the path, past the open grave, toward where she stood.

He wore a dress uniform, and despite the ocean breeze, the hillside climb was obviously a challenge for the still-recuperating man. Skye couldn't help admiring him. Despite the effort it obviously cost, he didn't falter, didn't miss a step.

Until he looked straight at her. He stopped, the grim smile on his face suddenly replaced with no expression at all. It was as if the sight of her meant nothing to him.

Why did that make Skye feel so sad? There was nothing between them. He didn't owe her a smile or anything else. She had chosen to save him. It had been her decision for reasons of her own—reasons she didn't fully understand herself. But whatever the rationale, he could never know what had actually happened.

"Officer Owens," shouted a well-dressed woman with a microphone in her hand. Her call started a frenzy of reporters vying for Trevor's attention. They all wanted a sound bite from him. Skye recognized some of the area's most famed news commentators, including Adrian Dellos, who was known for his criticisms of the ABPD.

Trevor stopped suddenly and turned to face the reporters who clamored to be noticed. With his back
toward Skye and her K-9 unit, he said in a voice so
low that Skye barely heard it, "Sorry, but no
comment, at least not today. We're here to celebrate
the life of a hero whose life was cut short. The
ceremony today will speak for itself."

That was probably the sound bite they were
panting for.

But Skye found it appropriate. Admirable. And a
little annoying. She didn't want to admire anything
about the man, or do anything else that might make
her feel closer to him. If that happened, she would
worry more about his recognizing what she was and
what she had done. Nevertheless, she found herself
watching his every move. Something about him
reminded her not only of being alive, but of being
very alive—of wanting to participate in all life had
to offer and of longing to do something about how
her body tingled just thinking about him.

Trevor turned then, ignoring further calls for his
attention, and soon reached her.

"Hello, Skye," he said. "Hell of a day, isn't it?"

"Sure is." She tried to find the right words of
sympathy for him, for his whole SWAT team, but by
then he was being greeted by the other K-9 officers.

"Good to see you," said Tritt. "When are you back on duty?"

"Not soon enough," Trevor said. "But I know what you guys are doing here. Any indication from your partners that Marinaro's present?"

He looked down at Bella and then up at Skye.

"Nothing yet," Skye said. "But we'll start patrolling when everyone's taken their places. If he's around, Bella will pick up his scent.

"Yes, I bet she will," Trevor said as Skye knelt beside Bella and gave her a big hug.

Why the hell did Trevor suddenly feel jealous of that dark dog with her tongue hanging out of her mouth? It surely wasn't because *he* could have started panting over the woman hugging the animal.

The woman filled out her dress uniform well. The thing shouldn't look sexy on her, but it did. Hell, everything probably looked sexy on her.

She stood again, glanced toward him, then looked quickly away, as if the activity along the hillside had once again captured all of her attention.

Maybe the idea germinating in his head was a bad one. He was considering teaming up with Skye after he was healed enough to do his job—*his* way. Her dog partner might have the best chance of ID'ing

Marinaro. But right now, all he should be thinking about was Wes being laid to rest.

A small band consisting of three bagpipers and a drummer marched into place near the grave site below. They played a sad, slow rendition of "Amazing Grace." Trevor steeled himself against an onrush of grief, then stared into the glistening, tear-filled blue eyes of Skye Rydell as she turned slowly, so slowly that she barely seemed to move—and looked at him.

Everything around him stopped. He was aware only of her. Her lovely, sad eyes watching him.

The world seemed to dissolve into a shimmering mistiness around him. It was as if he were asleep, dreaming, back in the warehouse where he had felt the bullet that penetrated his neck.

He again saw Wes Danver go down as his scream of pain abruptly stopped. Trevor felt himself shout, go after Wes—and get shot, too. Saw himself in some shimmering afterlife with Wes surrounded by light. He'd forgotten that at first, but now it had come back to him.

Had he seen Wes continue on, over a bridge? Toward the light? Was there a slender, sad woman walking with him?

No way. It wasn't possible. But he had seen those sad blue eyes of Skye Rydell's crying over him as he lay dying. He was certain of that. But had she really insisted that he live, drawn him back, away from that mist, away from Wes and the bridge?

"Hey, Owens, you okay?"

The sharp voice of Tritt penetrated Trevor's thoughts, bursting them as quickly as a blade stabbed into a balloon.

"Yeah," Trevor said. "Just don't like funerals, especially ones for friends." He looked abashedly toward Tritt.

"Look, you had a rough time. You coulda died, too. Maybe you ought to sit down for a while."

"I'm fine," Trevor insisted as Ken Vesco made his way over.

"Like Tritt said, sit down," he ordered. "Before you fall down."

Interesting that they seemed to give a damn about how he was doing, but Skye Rydell, who'd even visited him in the hospital, wasn't looking his way at all.

Of course, she'd come because he'd had Greg Blanding ask her. Greg was down below a little ways, standing on a grassy area with a bunch of other guys from their SWAT team.

Trevor should head there. Hang out with his real teammates. Get away from the dogs and their handlers.

Skye still wasn't looking at him. She seemed

tense, and her shoulders were shaking as she stared toward the mass of funeral attendees below.

A loudspeaker began to blare the service. The minister praised Wes, his courage, his life…and expressed great sorrow over his death.

Trevor didn't consider himself an emotional sort, but he felt his eyes mist, and he blinked. Damn! Now he really needed to get down the hill to his team.

But Skye was openly sobbing now. None of her own compatriots seemed to notice, or if they did they gave her no solace. At least she had her dog, who obviously sensed her grief. Bella sat so close to Skye's legs, nuzzling her, that she seemed attached.

It wasn't his job, but even so, Trevor drew closer to Skye. "You okay?" he whispered.

She nodded curtly, but as he repositioned himself at the side opposite Bella, he saw tears still streaming down her face.

Most women he'd seen crying got all red and puffy.

So how could Skye Rydell look so damned beautiful with the wetness bathing her skin, her blue eyes half shut in pain?

Almost instinctively, Trevor put his arm around her.

And just as instinctively, she leaned into him, put her head on his chest and shook as she wept even more.

Had she known Wes that well? Or was it the idea

of a funeral? A cop's funeral? Would she have cried this way if he, too, had died?

He tightened his arms around her. Skye pulled away.

"I'm sorry," she whispered. As he watched, she pulled a tissue from her pocket and wiped her face as she bent to hug her dog. She stood and watched stoically as the funeral continued.

Trevor wanted to keep holding her. Tight. No matter that he wasn't at all touchy-feely. He found her hot, but there was nothing sexual about this feeling of connection. Was there?

Enough of this. "See you later," he said in a low voice. "I've got to be with my team."

"Of course." The glance she gave him seemed poised now. Cool and remote, despite the tears still illuminating her eyes. "Thanks for your support, but I'm fine. I just hate funerals."

"Who doesn't?" He made himself hurry away at last, edging past tightly packed people as he headed downward.

His team greeted him silently, with nods and frowns that asked if he was okay. He gave them a thumbs-up and went to stand beside Greg Blanding.

Soon, the twenty-one-gun salute signaled the end of the funeral.

When the crowd began to disperse, Trevor

couldn't help glancing back up the hill, toward where the K-9 unit had stood. They, too, had scattered, probably allowing their dogs to meander through the throngs, seeing if they picked up the scents of any interesting suspects.

He didn't see Skye and Bella, which sent a pang of something through him. Not fear. He was never afraid. And it wasn't concern for her—not in this crowd. But...incompleteness? Need?

Hell, his damned near-death experience was turning him into some kind of woo-woo nut, yearning for who knew what. But he'd get over it, especially once he was back on duty, which he intended to be—soon.

As his team also started to disband, he saw Captain Boyd Franks motioning them all over.

Okay, he wasn't on duty, but that didn't mean he wasn't part of the group. He joined them.

"I'm running off to court now," the captain was saying. "The rest of you go back to the station and wait for orders, but I thought you'd be interested in knowing that the jury's being selected today for Eddy Edinger's trial. I won't be able to observe the whole thing, but I want to watch that murdering bastard squirm today, at least."

Maybe it was a good thing Trevor wasn't on duty just then.

He had a trial to watch.

Chapter 6

During the week after the funeral, tension ran particularly high at the ABPD. Irritability reigned, especially among the superior officers, who often snapped at their subordinates.

Skye worked hard at maintaining her cool, though. "Hey, Ken," she said after a particularly intense training session. They had worked in the grassy training area outside the station, just the two of them and their dogs.

The good thing was that crimes—at least crimes requiring K-9 assistance—were at a lull. The dogs trained in crowd control were called out to patrol highly attended sports events. They'd been taught to sniff out narcotics.

Unfortunately, genuine leads on the warehouse incident were few, and dwindling at that. Marinaro still remained at large. The entire department was on alert—and tempers grew short about what was perceived as a major failure.

"What?" Vesco snapped back at Skye.

"I think Bandit's a little confused—maybe getting some mixed signals. Let's give the dogs a rest, start again early tomorrow, okay?"

Vesco looked at her, sweat beading on his dark-complected face. He was clad in a bulky blue jacket with heavy padding that allowed dogs to attack without injuring their handlers. Vesco was essentially an okay cop. He got the message. "Sure thing." He clipped the lead on his partner and gave him a quick pat on the head. "Sorry, boy." He then looked at Skye. "Sorry, lady."

She grinned.

As she turned to head into the side door to the long, gray concrete building, she saw the captain at the main entrance. Trevor Owens was with him, and probably had been with him at court earlier in the day.

That was the other reason everyone was on edge. The murder trial of Eddy Edinger, a man arrested around the time Skye joined the department about eight months ago, was in progress. There had been delays in starting that had been engineered by the suspect's showboating lawyer. And from what she'd heard, the trial was not going well for the prosecution.

Trevor would return to active duty next week—which amazed everyone. Considering the extent of his injuries, that was a fast recovery.

Only Skye wasn't surprised.

He'd been around the station nearly every afternoon when court recessed. Skye had seen him around. Often. It was as if she was somehow drawn to him, whenever he was there. Or maybe he was drawn to her. She didn't always seek him out, but when they didn't run into each other in the hall, he seemed to drop in at her cubicle to say hi. Or he hung out and watched her training session with Bella.

Each time, he'd regard her with expressions she wished she could read. Sometimes he seemed quizzical. Other times she had a sense he wanted to tear her clothes off right there and engage in hot sex with her. Or maybe that was just wishful thinking on her part.

At least he didn't really know about her role in his survival. Anything he might remember now would have a dreamy, unreal quality to it. That's what Skye was always told by those in Minnesota whose lives were saved by others like her.

But the more time she spent with Trevor, the harder it might become to keep her secret.

"Come on, Bella," she told her dog. They'd go inside, change out of training gear, then go home—and avoid Trevor.

She still didn't know why Trevor attended the Edinger trial each day. He wasn't a witness. SWAT hadn't been called in during apprehension of that suspect. But the arrest had been difficult. Shots were fired and a bystander was injured. Edinger's alleged victims had been a real estate broker and a home owner. Edinger burglarized the house and then murdered the vics. The deaths had been especially brutal, as if the killer had wanted the victims to suffer. And it wasn't the first time this kind of murder had occurred—only the first time the suspect had been caught.

The buzz around the station was that the evidence against Edinger—who worked for the landscaping company that had been hired to spruce up the yard of the house, which was for sale—had been unassailable. He was absolutely guilty.

In the locker room, Skye changed from her dog training attire into civvies, with Bella keeping her company. She peered into the hall when she was dressed and saw several officers—none of whom was Trevor. Then she ducked into her cubicle and retrieved her purse and keys. "Okay, Bella," she said to her eager dog. "Let's go."

Although she was trying to avoid Trevor, she felt disappointed that he hadn't sought her out. Dumb, she told herself. She would run into him more than she wanted to when he was back on duty. She could fret then about his attitude toward her and toward what had happened at the warehouse. No need to punish herself now by seeing him any more than necessary.

Only…when she used the remote to open her K-9 black-and-white in the parking lot, she glanced toward the building—and there was Trevor, striding out. He looked good in his khaki trousers and light yellow shirt—a dressy enough outfit, she supposed, to be an observer in court.

But as he drew closer, she saw the thunderous expression that turned his well-defined features even sharper. Was he angry with her?

Bella was already in the back, and Skye started to get into the driver's seat, then stopped. He didn't even look in her direction.

Okay, she shouldn't feel hurt that he was ignoring her…but she did.

Plus, she was curious. If he wasn't upset with her, then why was he angry?

After she told Bella to stay and rolled down the windows a little for ventilation, Skye strolled in the direction Trevor was heading.

"Oh…hello, Skye." He seemed almost surprised to see her.

Searching for something neutral to say, she blurted out, "You're looking good, Trevor. I mean, healthier. You must be improving every day."

"Yeah. Thanks." Reaching a silver SUV, he stood beside it, his eyes finally focusing on her. His expression remained grim, and she forced herself not to cringe beneath it.

"Anything wrong?" she asked.

"You could say that." His tone suggested that whatever was going on was awful.

"Damn lawyers!" he exploded, slamming the side of a fist on the hood of his vehicle. "And damn our whole miserable legal system."

Oh. Something at the trial, then. But what would bother him this way? Quietly, she asked.

"The judge excluded some of the most important evidence against Edinger at the trial today. Said that it was gathered during an illegal search, that a warrant had been required because there were no exigent circumstances for the investigative team to take apart the vehicle. Not only that, but other evidence they found as a result of some paperwork that turned up…that's excluded, too. 'The fruit of the poisonous tree,' the lawyer called it—ever heard that expression? It means that if illegally seized evidence leads to further evidence, none of that evidence can be used against a suspect at trial. The prosecution's rested its case, the defense only has about a day of testimony, and then the thing will go to the jury without their being told some of the most damning stuff against Edinger. Damn lawyers!" he repeated.

"Oh," Skye said softly. "I didn't know you were so involved with this case."

"I wasn't. But I followed it, saw the extent of the evidence against this murdering slimeball, and now it looks like he'll walk. But not if I have anything to—" He stopped abruptly, then looked down at Skye blankly, as if he had taken strict control of his emotions. "Sorry. I'm just venting. Call me some kind of stupid idealist, but I really hate it when justice isn't done and murderers go free. Don't you?"

"Well…yes," she admitted, suddenly wrapped up in his utterly sexy and disarming smile. How had his mood changed so quickly?

And what was she doing here, talking with him?

"It's not so bad to be an idealist," she said gently, "except that for those in law enforcement, like we are, it's easy to become disillusioned. Justice doesn't always triumph, after all."

"Yeah, I got that," he said. "Well, anyway, maybe I'm wrong and the guy'll get what he deserves. Marinaro, too, whenever he's finally in custody. Look, I'm back on duty next week. We'll talk then. So far, the leads to that jerk haven't gotten anywhere, but I want to talk to you more about how Bella might be able to help find and apprehend that cop killer. What do you say?"

Under his winsome, sexually suggestive gaze, Skye suddenly thought she might wind up saying anything he wanted her to. Instead, she took control of herself—she hoped—and said, "I'm always willing to talk. But I'm not sure—"

"Good. I'll see you around before that, but maybe we can go out for lunch, coffee, whatever, to discuss it next week."

As they got into her car, Skye muttered to Bella, "Guess I blew that, didn't I, girl?" She was irritated with herself for not making it clear that she couldn't—wouldn't—work with Trevor that way.

Sure, she would love to help track down

Marinaro, and Bella was the greatest resource they had.

But being in Trevor's presence any more than she had to could only lead to trouble—especially if he started asking her more questions about why he didn't die in that warehouse.

Trevor sat in the driver's seat of his SUV, watching as Skye drove away.

Hell, maybe he was being too pushy. Just because her dog had once gotten Marinaro's scent didn't mean she'd necessarily find the SOB any faster than the rest of the guys in the department who were actively—and officially—looking.

But it gave him an excuse to talk to Skye. To stay in her presence, drink in how beautiful and sexy she was even while in uniform. To try to understand why he wanted to be with her so much. But there was something more. He sensed she might be able to help him figure out those odd hallucinatory memories he had of the day Marinaro shot him.

Almost unconsciously, he gently rubbed the side of his neck. Not surprisingly, it was still sore. It had only been a couple of weeks. And he could live with it.

What he couldn't live with was how dumb the legal system was. If the rest of the evidence wasn't enough, that jerk Edinger would get away with murder. Two murders. Because of a stupid legal technicality.

But not if Trevor had anything to say about it.

He started his engine, put the vehicle in gear and started driving slowly from the station. No use speeding and putting himself in danger.

He laughed aloud.

This was the first time he'd had two miserable suspects on his radar at the same time. And his way of dealing with lowlifes like that wasn't exactly designed to prolong his life.

He could have died at Marinaro's hand.

Once again, Skye Rydell's lovely face popped into his mind, as if she hovered over him. Crying. Somehow calling him back.

Hell, he had to do something about his overactive imagination. Maybe he could set it back on the path to reality if he spent more time with Skye. A lot more. Really got to know her.

In all ways.

That would definitely convince him she was one living, breathing, hot lady, completely separate from any woo-woo fantasy triggered by his near-death experience.

With that thought, he smiled slowly again, even as he had to shift in his seat.

For now, he'd settle for enlisting her assistance, hers and her dog's, in trying to track down the jerk who'd nearly killed him.

And maybe, just maybe, he'd figure out why he'd suddenly developed such a vivid imagination where Skye Rydell was concerned.

Chapter 7

On Tuesday morning, Skye parked her K-9 black-and-white in a space at the side of the station, leashed Bella and led her out the driver's door.

The station was near enough to the Pacific that the early morning haze had not yet burned off. It also muted the noise of traffic on the nearby freeway, giving the area an otherworldly aura.

But not quite the otherworld of Skye's heritage....

Her footsteps crunched on the pavement, while Bella's pattered alongside her. They'd been off duty on Sunday and Monday, and not much had happened on Saturday.

To Skye's chagrin, there still was nothing new in the search for Marinaro. To her relief, though, there had been no new major crimes requiring their presence, so they spent most of the last few days working on following scents and training to attack dangerous suspects.

They'd kept busy—a good thing. It kept Skye from thinking too hard about anything other than what they were doing. Otherwise, she'd do exactly as her mother and others with her abilities insisted should not be done: obsess over someone she had saved.

Not that she had any further doubts about whether she should have brought Trevor Owens back. She was certain now that she had done what was necessary.

What about him had made her decision so clear at the time? Other people who died still believed they had much to accomplish. But she had been so sure about Trevor's need to survive. Why? And what about him felt so compelling?

She had almost reached the door when Bella whined her need to visit the outdoor canine facility.

"Okay, girl." Skye changed directions.

All K-9 officers had the combination to the lock on the chain-link fence that enclosed the station's rear training yards. Skye opened the gate and Bella preceded her inside.

"Go on." Skye unleashed her partner. Bella loped off, sniffing the mown grass for the right location.

Seeing motion beyond the far side of the fence, Skye headed that way. Then stopped.

The field where humans trained was not empty. Only one person was there, though.

Trevor Owens.

He wore gray sweatpants and an Angeles Beach P.D. blue T-shirt and was obviously working out. Back in training—at a punishing pace, especially considering what he had recently gone through.

As Skye drew closer, he stopped doing push-ups on the grass and jumped to grab on to the high parallel bars, where he pulled himself up and straightened his arms. She could see the strain on his biceps as he again lowered and raised himself. His teeth were gritted, and his face glistened with perspiration in the misty air.

She felt a stirring of sexual sensation deep in her body. He was a hunk. But a lot of officers around here, especially those who trained hard for special operations like SWAT, kept themselves in shape. Sure, she noticed them. But she knew better than to allow herself to become attracted to any coworker—especially one who might have seen her using her special abilities.

But looking at this man surely wouldn't—

"Morning, Skye," said a voice to her left as Bella loped up beside her. She turned abruptly, mortified she'd been caught staring at Trevor Owens.

But it was just Ron standing there, in uniform and obviously reporting for the day's duty. He was smirking at her. "Admiring your handiwork?"

"Wish I could take credit," she joked. "But I think Officer Owens did it all himself."

"He's apparently not suffering any ill effects from his wounds." Ron narrowed his eyes teasingly. "Maybe you should go ask how he's feeling."

"I can tell how he's feeling," Skye said. "Better. You ready to go inside?"

"Sure am. I'm getting some special training in controlled substances today."

Skye knew that was a special interest of Ron's, and that Narcotics was one of several units within the department that he'd set his sights on. Back when they were in high school, a good friend of Ron's had OD'd on drugs, and he wanted to do what he could to put drug dealers behind bars.

"Great," she told him, then motioned for Bella to come along. They all headed to the station's rear door.

She let Ron precede her inside, then Bella. Skye stopped just for a moment to take a final look toward where Trevor Owens was still working out.

* * *

He'd seen her watching and decided, however stupid it made him feel, to ramp up the show.

Exhausted and panting, Trevor pulled himself up one final time, then dropped to the ground, bending forward from the waist, his body heaving with effort.

Slowly, he headed for his bag and pulled out a towel, using it to wipe his face. Then he looked toward the door where Skye had entered the station with Gollar and her dog. Stared for a long moment as if trying to see inside. See *her*. What was it about her that got to him this way?

It was time to put his fantasies far behind him. What he needed was to get himself back into as good a shape as before the shooting. He'd engaged in enough self-pity to last the rest of his career while stewing about the force's inability to find Marinaro. And then he'd watched the travesty of Edinger's trial.

The jury had gone into deliberations on Friday. No verdict yet. Maybe he was wrong about the system. Maybe the twelve jurors would see past the idiocy of the judicial system and make the right decision.

But without the excluded evidence…

There was no sense driving himself nuts. He headed inside for a shower. He stood under the stream of warm water for as long as he could stand it, then toweled himself off and headed back to get dressed.

"Hey, Trevor. You heard?" Captain Franks was in the locker room.

Trevor had a sinking feeling about why the captain was here. "Heard what, sir?" he asked quietly.

"Your buddy Edinger. Jury deliberated over the weekend and came back this morning."

Trevor grew very still, seeing the grimness on the captain's deeply lined face. "And?" he asked quietly.

"Acquittal. On all counts."

"Shit," he muttered.

"Yeah," replied Captain Franks.

By the time Skye slid into a seat in the station's sizeable roll call room, it was filled with fellow officers, male and female, from nearly all units. She liked this part of the day, when everyone starting their shifts seemed to be part of the same team—even if not everyone spoke much to one other.

Like the elite SWAT members. Those on duty always sat together at the back of the room and cracked jokes, or so she supposed since they always elbowed each other and laughed. She'd found this rather childish which was one reason she didn't go out of her way to talk to any of them. Besides, they

seldom deigned to do more than nod hello to an
ordinary K-9 officer like her.

"As if we're ordinary," she whispered into Bella's
ear, hugging her partner.

"What's that?" Ron asked from beside her, his
voice raised over the roar of conversation.

"Nothing." Adjusting her utility belt, Skye
glanced back again toward the SWAT enclave.
Trevor Owens hadn't come in yet, and she wondered why.

Almost as if she'd summoned him, he strode in the
door near the front of the room. He'd changed into
the fatigues of the SWAT team.

Captain Boyd Franks followed him. Neither
appeared happy.

"I wonder—" Skye said to Ron but immediately
grew quiet as the captain took his place at the
podium up front.

"Just a few announcements before you all run
off," he said.

Unsurprisingly, Trevor found a seat with the rest of
his SWAT unit, not sparing a glance in Skye's direction.

"First off, I want to welcome SWAT officer Trevor
Owens back to active duty," the captain said, the last
of his words drowned out by the cheering. "He's had
an amazing recovery," the captain finally continued,

"and we're proud of him. Next thing—a report and a warning."

Skye was appalled to hear that, as Trevor had feared, Edinger had been found not guilty.

"We'll hold review classes on probable cause for searches without a warrant," Captain Franks said grimly. "In my opinion, the detectives investigating Edinger made a judgment call that wasn't all bad, but after argument by the damned…er, the lawyers, the judge was convinced there wasn't probable cause or even exigent circumstances. We simply can't have that."

The room swelled with grumbling until the captain shushed them.

"On a brighter note," he said, "we received the report from the Force Investigation Division on our officer-involved shooting. Other than a reprimand for failing to apprehend the suspect on the spot, we're looking good. And on that subject—" He paused as if for dramatic effect. "We got what sounds like a good lead on Marinaro. A team's in the field even as we speak."

Skye was relieved. She wouldn't have to act upon Trevor's suggestion that he join forces with her and Bella to find the guy.

"I'm through here. Anybody else have something?"

No one did, and the captain dismissed them.

Despite herself, Skye was a little disappointed when Trevor, apparently engrossed in conversation with Greg Blanding, didn't even look in her direction as they filed out.

The hell with Owens. Her brief, intense acquaintance with the sexy SWAT officer was over. They were back to barely acknowledging each other's existence, which was fine with her.

What was it about that woman? When Trevor passed her, he thought he could smell her light yet intoxicating scent, even in this room filled with sweaty cops and a couple of dogs.

"So you're actually ready to go out in the field?" Greg asked, shaking his head. "You're really something. Superman, right? Or Spider-Man. Whatever, some kind of super guy who heals damned fast."

"Yeah, that's me." Trevor snorted derisively, but he knew what Greg was saying. He hadn't stopped wondering about it himself. He'd been so close to dying, had even given up. And now he was back on duty, a little sore, sure. Well, a lot sore. But definitely ready. He amazed even himself.

The vision of Skye Rydell bending over him when he was nearly gone—it just wouldn't leave his mind.

Maybe he was just experiencing a touch of wishful

thinking. He'd imagined himself with her in bed. Often. And out of bed. Against the wall. Wherever.

Even more now, when he felt so much better.

"Too bad about that Edinger trial," Greg grumbled as they walked through the crowded hall. "And now we have to go through more stuff on probable cause. As if we haven't already had more lessons on it than I can stand."

"Yeah," Trevor said, his mind back on reality at last. SWAT guys were at their best in the field. The book stuff like probable cause—other people should make sure it was okay before his teams were called in.

But it didn't always work like that.

SWAT hadn't been involved directly with the Edinger arrest, but Trevor had heard enough about it and seen enough of the evidence to know the guy was guilty of two really heinous murders. He'd ostensibly gone to do some landscaping at a high-end mansion that was on the market. He stole a lot of valuables and then murdered the real estate agent and home owner. Afterward, he'd hidden his cache in the trunk of his car and sped away.

The bodies had been found. A BOLO—Be On the Lookout—had been radioed, but the car and its driver hadn't been described. The neighborhood patrol cops had stopped him on a minor infraction and, acting on a hunch, checked his trunk. But the hunch was not sufficient legal justification.

A similar crime had occurred in another Angeles Beach neighborhood a few months before this one, and another in the same area a year before that. Edinger's work? Probably. And now he could do it again.

Or so he'd believe.

"Maybe we can be out in the field somewhere when those next classes are given," Greg said as they walked into the SWAT office.

"We can certainly try," Trevor said. He would definitely be out in the field a lot in the near future—especially while off duty. He knew right where he would be.

Right in Edinger's ugly, murdering face.

Chapter 8

A while after the roll call meeting ended, the K-9 unit received orders to respond to a burglary at a drugstore in an upscale area of Angeles Beach. Someone had broken in during the night and was tidy enough that the missing narcotics weren't discovered until an hour after the store opened.

An inside job? The detectives hoped that suspect-sniffing K-9s could help. Skye wondered if Ron would be sent out on this one. He'd want to help apprehend a suspect in a drug-related crime, but since he was a rookie his possible assignments at the scene would be limited.

"See you there in a few," Tritt told Skye as he raced out the door with his partner, Storm.

Skye quickly gathered her field equipment and clipped on Bella's leash. Her dog bounded eagerly beside her, obviously ready to go to work.

But their way was blocked by Trevor. A shiver of pleasure dashed through Skye, but she curbed her absurd reaction.

"You heard?" he said.

"Heard what?"

"Marinaro apparently struck again. Grabbed a coed in broad daylight as she drove onto the Angeles Beach University campus, but no one saw it, or at least no one paid attention and called it in. He forced his way into her car, and made her drive to the parking lot, where he assaulted and shot her. Pretty much his M.O. Only this one survived and, despite the severity of her injuries, she was able to call 911 and describe her assailant. SWAT's been called out in case he's still around, and K-9s are also about to—"

Captain Franks's graying head appeared over Trevor's shoulder. "You the only K-9 officer here now?"

She described the drugstore burglary offhandedly, hoping the captain would send her to the assault site instead.

"You'll do. See what you can do to trace Marinaro."

She forced herself not to smile in relief.

By the time Skye arrived at the scene, the three-story parking structure from which the victim had called had been emptied of civilians.

The victim had been transported to a hospital. There was no way for Skye to assess her condition— no way to help her at all, except to try to find the miserable SOB who'd harmed her.

The SWAT team swarmed the floor where the victim had been found. When they'd cleared it, Skye and Bella were brought in.

In case the suspect was still around, Bella had to do her stuff before the crime scene techs could enter to sift any evidence in the vehicle. The door to the sporty red SUV was forced open, and Skye gave her partner the command to follow the scent of whoever had sat in the driver's seat.

Once again, though, the trail ended quickly along the concrete floor, perhaps where another car, now stolen, had once been parked.

"Damn," Skye whispered to herself, then praised Bella aloud for doing a good job.

One of the suited detectives on the case brought her a bagged piece of clothing, which was taken from the car they believed to be Marinaro's. Skye had

Bella sniff it. The K-9 appeared to equate the two scents, smelling the shirt, then putting her nose down to the scent trail she had been following. This might help them in accusing Marinaro of both crimes, but Bella's "testimony" was not likely to be used to convict him.

Skye headed to the parking lot elevator with Bella.

"I know it was him, the bastard," Trevor muttered. She turned to look at him. He was in bulky gear that emphasized his physique and held his helmet along with his weapon. "That's what he does—although at least this time the victim may recover."

"What's her condition?" Skye hid her relief that her special abilities weren't required.

"Critical." She saw the pain on Trevor's face—as if he took personally the fact that his nemesis had struck again. She wanted to reach out to him. Soothe him somehow.

But she stayed still, motioning for Bella to do the same. If only she didn't work at the same station with Trevor. She'd feel a lot less pressure if she didn't have to be anywhere near him.

"Bad situation," she said levelly, treating Trevor as the professional colleague he was. "I hope the guy's apprehended fast. His hits are closer together now, aren't they? He's bound to make a mistake."

"Yeah, and I want to be there when he does."

"Looks like that won't happen today." She pushed the button for the elevator.

"How about grabbing dinner with me sometime soon?" he asked.

"I don't think so, but thanks."

"I want to discuss my idea of combining forces in an unofficial capacity. Tracking down Marinaro on our own—with Bella's help." He knelt to pat the dog, and Bella responded with wriggled pleasure. He looked up. "See, she votes yes."

Good thing none of their fellow officers was nearby. Fraternizing wasn't encouraged, although commanding officers were realistic. Men and women who worked together in intense, sometimes life-threatening situations often needed emotional release and camaraderie. But sexual fraternization was frowned on. It could lead to awkward moments, especially when an affair went bad.

Not that Skye considered this impulsive request a prelude to having sex with Trevor.

Of course she, of all people, understood why it was important to him to apprehend the man who had killed his superior officer and nearly ended his life, too. Plus, standard procedures had not, as yet, proven successful.

Could Bella and she really improve the odds? She

wouldn't know unless they tried. She was, after all, a cop, not just a Valkyrie. She had taken on this career because she believed in helping people and saving lives.

"All right," she said, wondering if she would regret the decision. "When would you like to get together?"

"Tomorrow night? There's something I need to do this evening." Whatever it was, Skye was sure, from the grim set to Trevor's well-defined features, that it wasn't going to be fun.

"Fine," she said. "Tomorrow night."

Too bad it couldn't have been tonight, Trevor thought with regret as he left the parking structure to catch up with the rest of his team. But what he intended to do this evening couldn't wait.

He got back to the station, showered and changed clothes, then started his official report of his participation in the search for Marinaro at the parking lot. He sat at his desk briefly, speeding through his report even as he planned his evening.

He hadn't been entirely surprised that Edinger was exonerated on a technicality. Justice was a fluid concept. On one hand, there was the official legal system. It decreed that a suspect was innocent until guilt was proven beyond a reasonable doubt and then created all sorts of ways to weasel around the facts so that doubt was practically a given. On the other hand, there was evidence. Facts. Reality.

Sure, sometimes they meshed. The guilty were actually found guilty now and then. And sometimes, innocent folks were convicted of crimes they did not commit. A shame? Sure. But what really got to Trevor was when those clearly guilty of really nasty crimes got off scot-free and were able to become repeat offenders who suffered no consequences.

He couldn't prevent that in all situations. No one could. But, one suspect at a time, he stopped as many as he was able.

He finished his report and sent it by e-mail to Carl Shavinsky, the acting team leader now that Wes Danver was gone. Then he left the station. His SUV was in the parking lot. He had changed into civilian clothes, so he didn't have to go home first.

He'd obtained copies of all the department's records on Edinger. He knew where the SOB lived and which landscaping service he worked for.

Edinger would know when a house's grounds were being spruced up for a sale and when the real estate broker was likely to be showing it to possible buyers. That was probably how he'd determined which home to rob. It would be open and there would be at least one person for Edinger to murder.

Trevor drove to where Edinger lived—a seedy residential area filled with crowded apartment buildings. Edinger rented a street-level flat at the front of one of the structures.

Trevor parked and walked up the broken pathway to the front of the building. There was no security system, so he continued through to the center courtyard, which looked surprisingly well maintained. Maybe the SOB tended it as partial payment of his rent.

Trevor heard a baby crying as he passed one apartment and an argument in a language he didn't recognize as he walked by another. Having scoped out the area, he finally reached Edinger's flat and knocked on the door. No answer. He tried again.

The guy either wasn't home or chose not to answer his door.

But just in case he hadn't yet returned from work, Trevor hurried back to his vehicle and headed for the office of the landscaping business, which was on a commercial street near downtown Angeles Beach. Trevor had checked. Edinger had kept his job while out on bail and was probably still employed now that he'd been found not guilty.

When he arrived, he recognized the black, seven-year-old cheap sedan from the description of Edinger's vehicle. The license plate matched, too.

Trevor parked and went inside.

Edinger was there, all right. He was surrounded by other guys in tattered work clothes and laughing his ass off. As he talked, he waved a can of beer. The others, too, were drinking.

"Yeah, I was worried." Edinger was obviously telling his story to his coworkers. "Who wouldn't be? I was out on bail, but I'd been in jail for a coupla nights getting processed and it was hell. I sure didn't want to go to prison. Thing is, you can't trust the damned lawyers, though mine seemed an okay guy. But—"

"But you got off, didn't you, Eddy?" Trevor asked in his most pleasant voice as he stopped in the doorway with arms folded. "A lucky thing, wasn't it?"

Confusion shrouded Edinger's rodentlike features. He had a big nose, buck teeth and a lot of scruffy brown hair. "Luck, hell," he finally crowed. "I got off 'cause I wasn't guilty. You're a cop, ain't you? I saw you in court, right?"

"Right, Eddy. And, yep, you weren't guilty in the eyes of the law. The evidence against you didn't stick. But we know all about real guilt versus real innocence. One of these days you'll slip up and I'll be there to kick your ass."

"Hey, you threatening me? I'm innocent, and no

one can make me go to trial again on those supposed murders."

The other people in the room, obviously his friends,
appeared ready to rally around Edinger.

"Gee, you know the law, Eddy. Very good. But, see,
there have been other unsolved robberies combined with
homicides that seem damned similar to the one you
just got off from. Maybe you can help me figure them
out while you fix up my yard." Now Trevor could truth-
fully state, if ever asked, that he had a quasi-legitimate
reason for being at this landscaping company.

"I ain't helping no damned cop," Edinger said belligerently. "Any of you guys going to help him?"

His friends clearly wouldn't and were ready to
rush Trevor, if Edinger gave the word.

"Fine." Trevor raised his hands as if in capitula-
tion. "I'll leave you all to your celebration this
evening. Enjoy it while you can. See you soon. Real
soon. Count on it."

And then, with a nasty smile on his face, Trevor left.

The game was afoot.

And he knew already how it would play out.

Although the dinner tomorrow night was strictly
business, the idea of it kept shooting the strangest,
most heated sensations through Skye's body.

She needed to keep her mind off it, so she'd gotten together with Hayley and Ron for drinks and salads on the outdoor patio of a beachfront restaurant. Kara was on duty tonight, so she couldn't come.

"You seemed distracted this evening, Skye," Hayley said as she munched on her last carrot stick. The resident trauma surgeon's ice-blond hair blew in the wind, wisping around a lovely face with prominent cheekbones and a petite nose. Her patients—the male ones at least—must believe they were being treated by an angel.

And they were, in a way, since Hayley, like Skye, had a special ability to deal with the dying.

"Distracted?"

"Yeah, thinking about Marinaro," Ron asserted. "That latest tip about Marinaro didn't pay off." He took his last swig of beer, thumping the glass down on the metal-mounted glass top of the table. Bella, who'd been sleeping beneath it, sat up and whined at Skye, who patted her head. "That damned cop killer is still out there somewhere."

"You got it," Skye agreed. "Everyone in the department is on full-time alert over that guy."

"We'll get him," Ron said. He wore a frayed U.S. Marines T-shirt, which was snug enough to show that he remained in well-honed physical condition.

His hair was too short to be tossed up in the breeze, but Skye's, like Hayley's, kept blowing into her face.

"We sure will," Skye agreed even as her mind, inevitably, returned to Trevor Owens.

"Anyway, got to run," Hayley said. "I'm on early morning duty at the hospital and need my beauty sleep."

As Hayley stood, the waitress came over with their bill and they split it three ways.

"See you both soon," Skye said. "Let's go, Bella."

As she drove along the boulevard lined with restaurants filled with patrons, she saw a sporty car speed by under the streetlights and start weaving in and out of the slow traffic.

She wasn't on duty, nor was she a patrol cop. Even so, she radioed the dispatcher. Just then she heard the sound of a horrible collision.

"Oh, no," Skye whispered. Her services would be needed this night, and not simply as a cop. She told the dispatcher to send emergency help and then parked along a red-painted curb, pulled out the ID she always kept with her and stuck it on the dashboard.

"Come on, Bella." She grabbed her dog's leash. As they ran down the crowded street, she heard the screams of horror and pain.

The faint, distant chanting inside her head told her that someone was mortally hurt.

The EMTs, who included Kara, arrived five minutes after Skye helped extract the injured from the piles of twisted rubble. The driver of the speeding car was unconscious. Possibly dying. So was the passenger in the other car.

Skye was furious, but the driver was a teenager. Too young to die. And as she touched his bloody arm to read him and determine whether or not to help him, she sensed he'd been speeding for a reason.

Kara glanced toward Skye as she hurried toward the other severely injured person. Moments later the pounding in Skye's head started again, followed by the familiar chanting of female voices. It grew stronger. She closed her eyes and saw a vision of the rainbow bridge. She was not on it this time, but Kara was there helping a beaming senior citizen to her destiny.

It had not been very long since Skye had saved Trevor Owens. The boy on the ground in front of her was almost as severely injured. Should she save him? It was time to decide.

She grasped his arm tighter. He opened his eyes, stared blankly and whispered unevenly, "Mom... Hospital... Is she okay?"

That was it. His reason for speeding. That poor family. He would die in moments if she did nothing.

And so: *It's not your time yet,* she told him silently. *You will live.*

As one of the EMTs bent over the young man, Skye suddenly felt a familiar exhaustion from saving his life by imparting to him a small part of her own life force. She also felt an impulse to return home to her family in Minnesota. There, she wouldn't be faced with these wearing, heartrending decisions so often. So inevitably.

"Don't even think about going home," Kara said firmly as if hearing Skye's thoughts. That wasn't one of their abilities…but they knew each other very well. "We do lots of good here. We save lives. You saved one tonight."

Trevor was across the street, watching from the shadows.

He had just left Edinger when he heard Skye's first call over the radio. Though off duty, he'd decided to see if he could help.

He'd arrived after the accident, around the same time as the EMTs who aided the injured. He had parked and rushed over, only to realize there was nothing for him to do but observe.

He was reminded somehow of the day he was shot—of waking briefly to see Skye bending over him.

Was the woman a masochist, intentionally putting herself in situations where people were injured, maybe dying?

Well, hell. She was a cop. Of course she'd be around murder and mayhem.

But still, there was something else he sensed about her and the way she acted around people who were injured. Something related to how she had somehow gotten beneath his skin?

Okay, maybe he just had a stick up his behind because he wasn't the only one hurt that she felt sorry for. *Jerk,* he told himself. But he wasn't convinced that was all.

He would find out more about her, and the odd stuff that kept yanking at him. Maybe not tomorrow, at dinner with her.

But he definitely would find out.

Chapter 9

Trevor arrived at the station the next morning before the early shift's roll call. He didn't want conversation till he'd had a cup of coffee, so he ran up the back steps to the second floor. There, in the blessedly empty kitchen, he punched buttons on a machine that brewed the hard stuff, full of caffeine. Grabbing his full ABPD mug, Trevor headed to the SWAT team office and sat at a worn wooden desk, booting up a computer. Fortunately, he was the only one there, although at least one other computer was on.

He had slept well the night before—but he'd have slept a lot better if he fully understood what he'd seen at that damned accident site.

He looked up Eddy Edinger's file. Trevor had the guy's home and work addresses, but hadn't found out if he had family around Angeles Beach. The computer file indicated he had a sister in nearby L.A. That might be useful. He printed the page.

"Hey, Owens. You're here early." It was Sergeant Carl Shavinsky, who'd been with SWAT since the beginning of time—or at least the creation of the ABPD SWAT team. Like Trevor, he was dressed for training. What was left of his hair was a graying stubble, and all the skin on his face, from beneath his eyes to under his chin, seemed to sag.

"Yeah. I couldn't wait to get back out there for another session of sweating and taking orders from you."

Shavinsky laughed. Then he turned serious. "You heard the latest about Marinaro?"

"The son of a bitch is dead?"

"Don't I wish?" Shavinsky took a seat behind the desk where the computer was already on. Despite the sagging of his face, his body was one of the fittest on the team, and that was saying something with this bunch. "No, the detectives following the latest anonymous leads came up with something yesterday, but it wasn't Marinaro, not directly."

"What was it indirectly?" Shavinsky had Trevor's attention.

"Looked like he might have been through his home after the last time our guys checked it out. There'd been messages on his answering machine that had been erased. He could have done it by pressing in codes from someplace else, but it doesn't matter. The detectives listened to them first and have been checking out the callers."

And maybe a K-9 sniffer should check out Marinaro's humble abode, to try to confirm whether those calls were listened to from away or from home. But a could a trained dog determine how recently the person leaving a scent had been there, or communicate it? No matter. It was still a possible excuse to get Skye Rydell involved.

"Great. See you at roll call," he said to Shavinsky. He'd had an idea who to talk to about capturing Skye's attention.

He headed for the crowded bull pen where patrol officers gathered and horsed around before roll call.

Trevor strode in as if this were his usual hangout. "Got a minute?" he said quietly to Gollar.

The short-haired rookie regarded him warily with chilly blue eyes. "Maybe. What's up?"

Trevor was about half a foot taller and had to bend a little so only Gollar could hear what he was about to say. "I need to talk to you about Rydell."

If Gollar had looked mistrustful before, now he appeared as suspicious as a prosecutor with a lying witness on the stand.

"I've asked her to work with me on finding Marinaro, and I need your input on how to talk to her without having her tell me exactly where to put my unofficial investigative ideas."

Gollar's expression softened. "Talking to Skye isn't hard," he began softly. "But getting her to go along with you is another matter." Then, seeing that others around them were watching, he said, "Hey, I need some coffee. Wanna join me?"

"Let's do it," Trevor said.

Skye hadn't slept well. Thoughts of yesterday's accident victims intertwined with uneasy dreams about her upcoming dinner with Trevor. She didn't always recall her dreams, but these had been vivid, filled with clever repartee and hot, sexy innuendoes that she would never, ever say in real life.

In any event, she'd been groggy on awakening

and was running late. She made it to roll call just in time. Fortunately, there were still a couple of seats left among her unit members.

"Decided to get some beauty sleep?" razzed Manny Igoa over the roar of voices, a grin splitting his long face. He sat tall in his folding chair as his dog, Rusty, sniffed a greeting to Bella.

"Not me, but you might try it someday," Skye teased back. She gave him a once-over and frowned as if dismayed by what she saw.

Beyond Igoa, Tritt laughed. "She's got you there, Manny." His K-9 partner, Storm, joined the other two on the floor beside the row of seats in the quickly filling room.

Her human cohorts had moved over, giving Skye the end seat. That put her nearest the dogs, so she held Bella's leash taut while keeping close watch on the others. She faced the open door when Ron walked in, neatly dressed in his navy ABPD uniform. There was a seat in front of her and she motioned to him to go there, but he seemed engrossed in conversation with someone behind him who hadn't yet rounded the corner. Someone taller.

Trevor Owens appeared in the doorway. To her knowledge, Ron and Trevor never conversed before, except, maybe, the way fellow officers generally acknowledged each other. But Ron wasn't SWAT, so he wasn't of interest to Trevor.

Or so she'd assumed.

Both nodded a greeting toward her. As they passed, Ron smiled, gave Bella a pat, and then moved on with Trevor, toward the back of the room.

Pretending to fuss with Bella's leash, Skye drew in her breath. What did Ron and Trevor have in common? And what were they talking about?

Trevor was almost amused at Ron Gollar's subdued excitement about getting to sit with the SWAT guys.

Oh, he hid it—or at least tried to. Trevor introduced the fit but naively fresh-faced cop to the other guys, though he probably knew most, if not all, the team members.

"Guys, you know Ron, don't you?" As always, they were poking fun at half the other cops in the room—and preparing gibes for the rest.

"Yeah, Gollar and I have met," Carl Shavinsky acknowledged, and gave a snide grin that lifted some of his many skin folds. "He carried some equipment out when I loaded the van the other day."

"Nice stuff," Ron said.

Just then Captain Boyd Franks appeared at the podium.

"The chief looks pissed," Ron said.

"Sure does," Trevor agreed. While pretending to focus his entire attention on the chief, whose scowl deepened as he thumbed through the pages he had brought to the podium, Trevor looked sidelong toward the person on the end seat in the fifth row.

Of course he had noticed Skye the instant he'd walked into the room. Although he had pretended not to see the distractingly gorgeous K-9 officer, he had noted her curious and somewhat displeased glare as he and her buddy Gollar walked toward the back of the room.

She seemed to be having a hell of a good time, animatedly talking to her fellow K-9 officers. She turned sideways a lot, giving Trevor a good view of her luscious profile.

"Okay, everyone." Captain Franks's creaky but loud voice reverberated as he spoke into the microphone. "Before we begin our morning's official agenda, I want to mention to you again the department's concern about how Edinger got off on a technicality. We're still working on scheduling a mandatory class on Fourth Amendment rights and what constitutes an illegal search and seizure, but until we do, I want to give all of you some reminders."

Fourth Amendment rights. What about victims'

rights? Trevor wondered. And not just in this case, but in the other similar, unsolved cases that were probably also Edinger's handiwork. With the scumbag of a suspect on the loose, innocent citizens were placed in unnecessary danger.

Trevor would attend the mandatory class, of course. Give lip service to Fourth Amendment rights, getting warrants when needed, whatever.

But he'd do so while handling the situation himself. His own way.

Chapter 10

After roll call, Skye wanted to work off her frustration and so was glad when Curt Tritt decided they all needed a major K-9 training session.

She led Bella outside to where the other dogs were already lined up with their handlers. Ken Vesco and Bandit had arrived after an early-morning veterinary checkup. Now the two were leading the training maneuvers, with other officers working their dogs accordingly. They mostly had different specialties. Bandit's was to scent out drugs and contraband, Rusty's was crowd control and Bella's and Storm's was to track suspects at crime scenes. Fortunately, the ABPD's brass believed in versatility, so they all trained in areas besides their primary ones.

Today's exercises consisted of working with the dogs on the attack command. Each took turns assaulting its trainer's arms, which were covered in bulky protective gear.

Igoa started the exercise. After his shepherd wrestled him to the ground, it was her turn. "Attack, Bella!" she commanded.

Bella did so magnificently, wrestling a struggling yet cooperative Skye onto the grass, stepping on her to hold her down and placing her muzzle gently against her neck. In a situation where a real suspect was being subdued, Bella would bare her teeth and growl.

"Relax," Skye commanded.

She put Bella through another exercise. When done, she glanced toward the doorway into the station—and there stood Trevor, watching. Skye felt a frisson of pleasure, glad they'd done things so well while being observed.

But after nodding at her, he disappeared back inside, which left her feeling confused and ill at ease.

Trevor had paperwork to do before heading to the firing range for practice. He still felt stiff and wanted to be sure his marksmanship wasn't affected.

But as he walked through the halls toward the SWAT office, all he could think about was Skye. He was drawn to the smooth, graceful way she moved, her loving firmness with her K-9 partner and her empathy about Edinger's release and the department's inability to locate Marinaro. He would use it to appeal to her, to make sure she agreed to use her dog to locate Marinaro. But that would be later.

It was only midmorning. He had hours before his one-on-one with Skye. Well, one-on-two, since she'd bring Bella.

But, as it turned out, dinner with Skye and Bella wasn't in the cards that night.

When he returned to the station late in the afternoon after a stint at the off-site firing range, he got a call on his radio. "All SWAT officers," boomed Shavinsky's voice. "Call out to a possible crime scene. A 911 came in from a female, age unknown, who claimed someone's stalking her." His tone grew gruffer, as if he spoke through clenched teeth. "Sounds like a possible episode with our buddy Marinaro, guys. Let's get him."

Hell. Trevor'd had every intention of working on Marinaro's case that night—his way. The thought that the SOB might have harmed another woman made him clench his fists.

He *would* bring the guy down…. If not tonight, via official means, then by using whatever it took.

No way would this creep continue his murderous rampage.

Skye shuddered as she stood outside the charming beaux arts–style theater where Marinaro was supposedly holed up with his latest victim, a young woman who had managed to call 911.

Was she still alive? No one had heard from her again.

She was an actress affiliated with the thespian group that put on plays in this historic theater. That's what some of her friends and coworkers who'd shown up to gawk had said. They were now kept back beyond the crime scene tape. Skye remained with Bella, who whined as she obediently continued to sit on the sidewalk.

Skye remained alert, ready to give Bella the command to search for a suspect the moment she herself received orders to move.

For now, it was up to SWAT yet again. They were preparing for their dynamic entry. Hopefully, they would not be too late to save the woman.

The nearby street was filled with black-and-whites, their occupants squatting behind them in case shots were fired. The big, boxy SWAT van was right up front. The crime scene perimeter stretched way beyond the block, with officers holding back the crowd. The sound of police and media helicopters filled the air. So did excited shouts.

The SWAT team members were all geared up, clad in their protective clothing, assault rifles and semiautomatics at the ready.

What would happen if this suspect once again opened fire?

What if someone on the SWAT team was hit?

If Trevor was hit again?

Could she save a victim more than once?

"I don't even want to think about it," she whispered to Bella.

"You okay, Skye?" Ron was suddenly at her side. He, too, had been called out to this site, assigned to work crowd control. Of all the people here, only he would have a sense of what she was going through.

Not all of it, though. He couldn't possibly know how scared she was for Trevor's sake, how she feared she would be unable to help him if things went bad.

"This waiting's getting to me," was all she admitted.

It appeared Ron felt the same way. He looked pasty against the deep blue of his uniform. "We need a win against the bad guys here," he said firmly.

And then—flash! Bang! The door to the theater was battered down. The SWAT team burst in.

No sound of shots fired. Thank heavens!

Maybe this was a false alarm.

And then…the syncopated banging of gunshots resonated from somewhere inside. Oh, Lord, were any SWAT guys down? Skye had no sense of anyone hit. No chanting filled her head.

More shots… Loud. Assault weapons fired. "Officer down!" came the shout over the radio.

No additional gunfire. Time for her to go in with Bella. Track the suspect. Act by instinct. Once more, she could not wait for official orders.

But which officer was down?

This time, Skye wasn't alone. She had her gun drawn as Bella and she cautiously entered the premises with Curt Tritt and Storm.

What would they find inside?

The good thing was that she still heard no chanting in her mind. No telling how badly injured the downed officer was, but for this moment, at least, he wasn't dead. Or even close to dying.

Skye and Tritt entered the picturesque old theater's velvet-trimmed lobby cautiously, dogs at their sides. Last time she'd been called out to a similar scene,

Skye hadn't had time to grab a K-9 ballistics vest from the station to protect Bella.

This time, both Bella and Storm wore vests.

None of the SWAT members was in the lobby. Tritt spoke into his radio. "K-9 units 2 and 9 here. Need instructions. Anyone see the suspect? Over."

"Come inside the theater," said a half-garbled voice Skye didn't recognize. "We got a weapon here you can use for scenting. Over."

A weapon. One the suspect, Marinaro, must have handled. Did that mean he was unarmed now? She prayed that was so.

But where was he?

Which officer was down?

She found out quickly after Tritt and she entered the auditorium from the back, behind the plentiful tiers of seats. It was a lovely old place, complete with crystal chandeliers and carved wooden balconies.

Nothing as horrible as a shooting should occur here—unless it was fake stuff, onstage.

Tritt and she hurried down the aisle with their dogs. Shavinsky had been hit in the shoulder. He sat at the edge of the stage. The room had been cleared, and a couple of other SWAT guys were seeing to his wound until the EMTs could get there.

Where was Trevor?

And the woman who'd made the original call? "Has anyone found the victim who called 911?" Skye asked.

"Not yet." Shavinsky shook his head slowly. His color wasn't good. Skye hoped the EMTs got to him before the trauma caused any further injury—like a heart attack. "The other guys went to look for her in the dressing rooms behind the stage."

That must be where Trevor was. Unless, of course, he followed Marinaro—a possibility that made Skye cringe inside.

"Curt, why don't you see if Storm can follow the suspect from the scent on the weapon he was handling? I'll take Bella to try to find the victim."

Tritt agreed, and one of the SWAT guys worked with him, showing him the vicious-looking handgun now in a plastic evidence bag.

Skye led Bella up stairs at stage right, then behind painted scenery that resembled a meadow till she found a door. Her hand on her weapon, Skye slowly pushed open the door.

No sounds, and no reaction from Bella indicating that she sensed anyone's presence.

The hallway was dimly lit at the floor level, probably what was used when a play was going on. Skye motioned for Bella to stay at her side. She heard nothing, but Bella did. The dog stood at attention and stared down the hall, her pointed ears moving like active antennae.

"Go," Skye whispered.

Bella led her to the farthest door. It was closed. Bringing her gun hand again to firing position, Skye waited a moment, then slowly tried the knob. It didn't turn, but now Skye, too, heard a muffled sound from inside.

The suspect?

After giving hand signals that told Bella to stay, Skye raised her leg and thrust it hard at the door, praying it was as flimsy as it appeared. It opened hard, slamming against the wall at the far side. Half expecting gunshots to fly into the hallway, Skye ducked as she both aimed her weapon and blocked Bella.

Nothing—except for more muffled noises.

After looping Bella's leash around her wrist, her other hand still grasping the Glock, Skye entered.

Still moving cautiously, she reached for a switch on the wall. In a moment, light flooded the room— revealing a half-clad woman lying there. Something was tied around her mouth. "Officer requests backup," she said into her radio, describing where she was. "I've located the victim."

* * *

Fifteen minutes later, the woman was draped in towels and was hysterically describing what had happened. Several officers had joined Skye to listen. Her attacker definitely sounded like Marinaro. Her fearful 911 call, which she made before he'd grabbed her, probably saved her life, since he'd had time only to sexually assault her before hearing the flash-bang entry of the SWAT team. He'd worn gloves, a mask and a condom, so she wouldn't necessarily be able to ID him and DNA evidence might also be inconclusive. He had bound and gagged her, and he'd left the room.

"Do you know where he's gone?" Skye asked.

"No," wailed the woman. "I think he came in through the tunnel to the parking lot that the actors and stagehands always use. He may have gone back that way."

Along with other officers including Ron, Skye headed, with Bella, back into the hall. She determined to take Bella and follow the directions the victim had given for finding the tunnel.

"Hey, Gollar," said Ron's partner, Jim Herman, when they were near that backstage area. "Let's go at this the other way. Come with me to the parking garage."

"Roger." Ron started after him, then stopped. "Tritt will come with you, okay, Skye?"

"I'm fine," she told him. And mostly, she was. But she couldn't help wondering where Marinaro had gotten to—and whether Trevor had already found him.

The fact she'd heard no more gunshots was a good thing...wasn't it?

Bella pulled on her leash. "Go ahead, girl," Skye encouraged.

Bella led her down the way she'd come, from the stage area, as Tritt and Igoa went the other way. But instead of turning right, Bella pulled left, to a jog in the hallway.

Behind a protrusion in the wall was a door. To the tunnel?

As cautiously as her training had taught her, Skye again unholstered her weapon and prepared to go through the door.

Then a volley of gunfire sounded. Some of the shots came from an assault rifle. Trevor's?

Skye turned the knob and thrust the door open. She grabbed Bella and pushed her out of the way, bracing her own back against the wall.

Nothing.

Except for a low, keening chant inside her head.

Someone was injured. Seriously. Who? She wouldn't know until she reached the scene.

Not Trevor. It couldn't be Trevor.

The hallway was well illuminated by recessed lights in the beige plaster ceiling. Its floor was a pattern of brown and white vinyl squares.

No one appeared along its length.

Cautiously, Skye darted along it. When she reached the end, she saw an open doorway to her left. No one was visible, but the doorway appeared to lead into the parking lot.

Still grasping Bella's leash, she hurried that way—and heard the radio at her belt crackle. No time to respond. She turned the corner—and there was Trevor. Kneeling on the floor of the parking lot.

"No!" she cried, rushing to him even as the pounding, the chanting, swelled and engulfed her mind. Bella barked, staying with her.

"Skye, I missed him, damn it." Trevor looked up grimly. A middle-aged man in a suit was crumpled on the floor, blood pooling beneath his head. "He shot this civilian—to distract me. He's not breathing. I've started chest compressions and called for the EMTs." Trevor recommenced the CPR.

Skye closed her eyes. Her mind filled with the vision of the man on the rainbow bridge. She knelt beside Trevor and reached for the man's hand. Now she saw herself join the victim, who was shouting in her mind. "No. Not now. My kids! My wife."

"I'm so sorry," Skye whispered. Could she bring him back? No. She couldn't, and it hurt her. He was too far gone, shot in the back of the head. No way could he survive. Skye quickly steeled herself, swallowed her sorrow. What she *could* do was to see that he made it over the bridge, to a comfortable eternity.

"It will be all right. You'll see." She held on for another minute, and then the figure on the bridge relaxed, giving in to the inevitable.

"Thank you," he said brokenly. "It wasn't your fault. I'll be fine. I can feel it."

Tears filled Skye's eyes in her vision—and in reality. She felt them spill over her cheeks, even as she opened them and found Trevor, who was no longer giving CPR, staring at her. His hand was touching the man's neck as though seeking a pulse, and he looked at her with concern—and curiosity.

"He's gone," Trevor said. "What the hell were you—"

But before he could say anything else, Skye dove into his arms, which opened reflexively. She held him. Tightly. "It's so sad," she cried.

He drew her to her feet. She looked up to find him still staring...but this time there was more in his gaze. Something heated. Something incredibly suggestive and sensual. She realized how closely their bodies were fitted together.

They were alive.

And suddenly, but as if they had been waiting forever for this moment, she strained upward and he complied, covering her mouth in a hot and welcome kiss.

Chapter 11

Ghoulish? Hell, maybe it was, to be standing here in a public parking lot, lip-locked over the newly deceased body of this civilian. But he didn't stop. No way.

Her sweet, sweet lips on his, burning them. Burning every inch of him as he pressed against her soft curves and ached for more. It was all he could do not to grind his growing erection against her. But she felt it and pushed toward him, as if she wanted to join him. Be part of him.

He wanted more. Lots more. No way was he ending this kiss. Not this fast. If only they were alone, someplace private. Someplace where gasoline fumes and oil and mustiness weren't mixing with the soft, floral scent of her.

Then he could pull off her uniform. His uniform.

But they were on duty. This was wrong...for now. Even so, he reveled in the sensations of her mouth, her tongue, against his.

Ghoulish? This was a celebration of life. His life, for he had almost died a couple of weeks ago. And Skye—had she helped to bring him back? The hell if he knew. She could just have been messing with his mind the way she was now messing with his body and all its sensations.

"Trevor," she murmured against his mouth, pulling back a little. Her beautiful blue eyes opened, looking both dazed and shocked at the same time. "We can't... This isn't..."

Bella suddenly barked, and Trevor heard footsteps running in their direction. "Damn," he muttered. Within seconds, Skye was several feet away and focusing her attention on her noisy dog.

That gave him time to stick his hands in his pockets and rearrange the fit of his pants that had grown so tight so quickly.

"Hey, Skye, Trevor, you okay?" Ron Gollar joined

them, along with Jim Herman. "I heard the EMTs outside. They're coming in, if we're clear."

"Yeah, we're clear," Trevor growled. "This vic was down before Skye and I got inside, and no sign of the suspect. Best I can judge, we need the coroner, not the medics, but we'll let them figure that out."

"Too bad," Herman said sadly. The tall African-American clenched his fists like he was ready to punch someone. Trevor had seen the former football star train. He wouldn't want to be on the wrong end of those fists.

"Tell me about it." Now that he'd come to his senses, Trevor was pissed. Marinaro had gotten away. Again.

And he'd let his guard down with Skye. Way down. Sure, she was one sexy lady, but she was a fellow cop, and they were on duty.

He hazarded a glance toward her, but she wasn't looking his way. Everything else—her dog, their fellow officers, her gear, the parked cars—seemed to capture her attention, diverting it away from him. To his own amazement, he had to chomp down on a smile. She was embarrassed, when there was no need. No one had seen them. No one knew…but them.

The EMTs dashed inside the parking lot, lugging their equipment. A woman was the first to kneel on the floor and check the victim's throat and wrist.

"No pulse," she asserted. Immediately, she began chest compressions, while her partner readied an oxygen mask to put over the victim's face in case he began breathing. "Nothing," she soon panted, then started thumping on the man's chest.

As the medics worked, Trevor thought about how Skye appeared when he was dying—how she knelt over him, wept and demanded his return to life.

Didn't she? He remembered that now—or was it a false memory?

Then there was that car accident. She had treated the teenage boy the same way. There was something unusual about Skye's connection to life-and-death situations. Somehow she seemed to participate in them.

Some people died, like this victim, and Wes Danver.

Some lived…like Trevor himself.

Did any of this have to do with Skye? Or was he imagining it?

"He's gone," said one of the EMTs.

A bunch of fellow cops, including Tritt, had arrived here. As it had been in the theater, onlookers were being kept out.

"Did you find the suspect, Curt?" Skye sounded anxious.

"No," the senior officer said angrily. "Storm

tracked him along another underground passageway, into an alley and then stopped. He must have had another vehicle there, or stole one."

Like last time. Marinaro must plan his locations carefully. But Trevor knew that now, as did the rest of the ABPD. They would know better how to handle it next time.

There would be a next time, no doubt about that.

Now Trevor had even more impetus to reschedule the dinner with Skye. Follow-up and reports would prevent it tonight. But he had more questions than ever. And if they happened to share another kiss— hell, a lot more than kissing—that would be a good thing. His body tightened at the idea.

Or would she renege now?

His fellow SWAT officers who'd dashed into the parking lot were starting to disperse. He needed to go with them, but first he headed toward Skye.

She looked up at him, her expression studiously bland…and her cheeks an adorable pink.

"Sorry we missed out on dinner tonight," he said in a low voice. "How's tomorrow?"

She looked for an instant as if she was considering telling him where to go. But then she took a deep breath, met his eyes and smiled briefly. "Fine," she said.

* * *

What the heck was she thinking? Skye wondered that for the rest of the evening, first back at the station as she started her report on what had gone down and then when Bella and she returned home.

She should have taken advantage of the reprieve and not accepted Trevor's latest invitation. Hell, she should stay as far away from him as possible.

Especially after that kiss. While taking her shower, she kept thinking about how their kiss had seared through all of her most vital organs. How she wanted more.

She had seen him gaze at her when the paramedics worked on that poor victim and could tell he was re-membering his own near-death experience, and her presence there.

But despite all her self-admonishments, she had to admit she looked forward to seeing him tomorrow. It wasn't sex-driven…well, not entirely. She wanted to help catch that awful suspect, Marinaro, too.

Edinger was a lot easier to locate than Marinaro. Why shouldn't he be? A jury had found him not guilty. He must still feel home free—at least till he killed again.

Trevor planned to stick to him like an extra appendage. Wait him out. Goad him, till he exploded.

Guys like that always did.

This time Trevor decided to confront him on his home turf.

The lights were out in Edinger's first-floor apartment in this run-down neighborhood where most streetlights were broken—maybe shot out to ensure that sidewalk transactions went down without illumination.

The fact that Edinger's place was as dark as the rest of the surroundings didn't mean he wasn't around. It was four o'clock in the morning.

Trevor pulled out a limited-use cell phone he'd bought for this purpose and called Edinger's home number. It rang three times before he heard the click of someone picking up.

"Yeah?" came the croaked response. "Who's this?"

"Good morning, Eddy," Trevor said cheerfully. "How about a little guessing game? Who do you think this is?"

A pause. Then— "Go to hell, you dickhead cop." Edinger slammed down the phone, which only made Trevor grin all the more.

He pressed the redial button, but this time got a mechanical voice telling him to leave a message.

He didn't—although he figured Eddy got the message anyway.

Next, he called Eddy's cell phone number. Again, the guy didn't pick up. Big surprise. When the voice mail came on, he left a message.

"Hello, Mr. Edinger," he said in a hearty voice. "Rise and shine. And if you really want to get a great start to your day, look out your window. See that SUV across the street—the only one around here that isn't all banged up? If you look real hard, even with no lights on out here, you'll see it's occupied. By me." He did not give his name, of course. "I've got an eye on you. Both eyes. I'd suggest you put on your halo and act like a perfect angel. Not even bump into another person, let alone kill one. Otherwise, you're really going down, Eddy. Oh, and in case anyone asks, the real purpose for this call is because I'm worried about your health, after all you've gone through, so I'm watching out for you. Take good care of yourself, and have a great day."

Trevor hung up and waited—behind a tree in case Eddy had a long-range weapon and was upset enough to be trigger-happy.

He grinned a lot more when he saw lights go on in Eddy's apartment, then go off again. Were the drapes in the front window moving? Yeah. Trevor couldn't quite make out the shape of who was standing there. Edinger used the curtains to cover him, thought they'd be some protection.

Trevor waited a little longer, and when Eddy neither came out nor shot at him, he slipped back into his vehicle. He turned the key in his ignition, revving the engine before putting the SUV in gear. He drove a few apartment buildings down before turning around and double-parking in front of Eddy's apartment.

He blinked his headlights, tapped his horn three times and then drove off.

A few hours later, Trevor yawned as he printed his report about yesterday's events and stretched out as best he could in the chair in his cubicle at the station.

"You finished?" Greg Blanding called out from a nearby desk. Like Trevor, he'd come in way early, before day shift roll call, and had just e-mailed his report.

"Yeah, I'm done," he told Greg. "And, yes, before you ask, I feel good enough to head outside for a workout." But the question he'd known his thin friend with the shaved head was about to ask reminded him of his injuries. He instinctively rubbed his neck. It was still sore, but he was getting close to a hundred percent.

"Good," Greg said. "Shavinsky's back on duty already. Almost as amazing as your recovery… Well, not quite. His wounds last night weren't as bad as yours. But he's mad. Wants to talk to us before roll call, get us ready to run some practice scenarios later on, probably similar to those we've already encountered with Marinaro."

Trevor thought practice scenarios like that would make damned good use of K-9s with certain training backgrounds, but he wasn't going to bring that up just yet.

"Is Shavinsky officially our team leader yet?" he asked as he stood up. He'd come to the station wearing workout sweats in anticipation of the exercises to come.

"Any day now, or at least that's the way the guys who've chipped in to our pool see it. We're each choosing a day as the one we think the final decision will be announced. You want in?"

"Why not?" Trevor reached into his pocket and pulled a ten-dollar bill from his wallet. "Who's keeping it?"

"Yours truly. We're all bought out up to next Monday. You want then?"

"If that's the best I can do."

They headed outside. Trevor's gaze instinctively

went toward the fenced area next to the SWAT training grounds where the K-9s hung out for their workouts and other needs. A couple of guys were there doing early morning exercises with their dogs, but not Skye and Bella, which was probably a good thing since Trevor wanted to concentrate on the training exercise he was about to engage in.

About half the team was already there. Most were doing push-ups and pull-ups to prepare themselves for the day's official training. Before Trevor could join them, his new cell phone rang, and he pulled it from another pocket. He recognized the number on the display. "Owens," he barked.

"Hey, Owens, this is Edinger. I want you to know I talked to my lawyer, and he said your calling me in the middle of the night, showing up where I work—that's harassment. I can sue you and your damned police department for millions if you don't lay off. Got it?"

"Well, gee, Eddy. I think any claim you'd make would be your word against mine. I showed up at your work establishment because I'm thinking of having some landscaping done at my house and I'm starting to think about who to hire. And any other call I might have made to you—which I'm not confirming—would have been simply to check on your welfare."

"Look, just leave me alone. I'm not guilty. Just ask the judge. Got it?"

"I got that you got off," Trevor said with a tight grin. "Not that the system did what it was supposed to. So, good guy that I am, I'll watch your back—a lot. Make sure you're safe. Same goes for everyone around you. Of course if you get out of line and try to kill someone else, just remember I'm right behind you. And I'll catch you in the act. Then we'll see if some high and mighty judge will let you off on some ridiculous technicality. See ya, Edinger." Trevor hung up.

The guy really was getting a little nervous.

What a shame.

Chapter 12

Yesterday's surviving victim was going to be fine. She had been held overnight in the hospital for observation, and Skye had gone to see her before reporting for work.

Her name was Sally Brighton, and she was twenty-five years old, only two years younger than Skye. At the theater, her long hair had been disheveled and her face was a mask of terror. This morning she sat in the hospital bed wearing a frilly pink robe that was probably her own. Her dark brown hair was combed in attractive waves about her pretty, small-featured face. There was a haunted look behind her amber eyes, even though she smiled at Skye.

"You were there yesterday," she said immediately after Skye knocked and entered the room.

Since she would soon be on her way to the station, Skye wore her uniform, and her hair was pulled away from her face as usual. Though she figured she looked like a cop, she was a little surprised that the woman recognized her, considering the state of panic she'd been in at the time they'd met.

"Yes, I was there," Skye acknowledged. And maybe she shouldn't be *here*. But she cared about what happened to this woman.

And she wanted to learn all she could about Marinaro to assist in stopping him from hurting anyone else.

"You had a dog with you, didn't you? I have to say that things yesterday… Well, I remember more than I want, but not all I should." A frown creased her otherwise perfect complexion.

"You'll recall everything that matters, I'm sure. You've been interviewed already by some detectives, haven't you?" The ABPD detectives were always efficient, but Skye didn't want to taint anything by her own questions if, for some odd reason, they hadn't yet spoken with her.

Sally confirmed that she'd been interviewed several times—in the ambulance, after she'd been treated at the hospital and early that morning.

"I'm so sorry this happened to you." Skye approached the stark hospital bed, where Sally looked almost too exhausted to be propped into a sitting position. "And I'm not asking right now in any official capacity, but can you describe who hurt you?"

Skye knew full well what Trevor Owens had in mind to discuss that night at dinner. She wanted to come prepared. And ready to work with him—but only if it made sense.

"It never dawned on me that I shouldn't be there alone," Sally said with a shudder. "The theater's like my second home. And when I heard someone come in, I assumed...I assumed it was another cast member, or someone else associated with our acting troupe." Tears started cascading down her smooth cheeks.

And when she gave a description of her attacker that matched Marinaro's, Skye nodded but didn't mention his name.

"Thanks for going back over such a hard thing," she said softly. "Everything you tell us will hopefully help us catch the suspect quickly and prevent him from hurting anyone else."

"He killed a man last night, didn't he?" Sally

cried. "They didn't tell me here, but I saw it on the news." She waved her hand toward the television mounted on the wall facing her bed.

"Unfortunately, he did kill someone in the parking lot," Skye confirmed to the weeping woman. "Was he... Did you know him?"

"No. They said he was just there to see if he could get tickets for his family for this weekend's show." Sally started crying even harder, and a nurse came in.

"I'm sorry, Officer, but I have to ask you to leave," she said. "Ms. Brighton needs her rest."

"Of course. Please take good care of her. And, Sally, please know that I—we—will do all we can to find the man who hurt you."

Skye hurried out the door and rushed home to pick up Bella, so they wouldn't be late for roll call.

She wanted to see Trevor this morning, first thing—to confirm their dinner meeting tonight and let him know she was ready to offer her services and Bella's to catch Marinaro.

"I thought Marinaro might strike again this evening to make us postpone again," Trevor said. "He's got to know that once we've teamed up, he's toast." He grinned, and she smiled back.

Trevor sat across the table from Skye at one of the

area's most posh restaurants, the Angeles Fish House. He had called earlier, and she had agreed, reluctantly, to leave Bella home. This place was worth an evening away from her partner. Every table in the dimly lit dining room was occupied, but the acoustics were good enough, despite the violinist playing softly in a corner, for Skye to hear Trevor's every word.

Or maybe it was because she concentrated on him so deeply.

"I'll drink to that." She lifted her wine goblet.

Trevor clinked his goblet against hers, then took a sip. He wore a beige button-down shirt that, even in the soft lighting, seemed to deepen the dark mahogany shade of his eyes. Their sparkle was enhanced even more by the twinkling candle in a frosted glass holder.

Skye tamped down her simmering sexual reaction. This was business. "I went to see last night's victim, the woman who survived," she told him. She described her visit as the mellowness on Trevor's face slowly turned into a frown of concern. But as expressive as his face was, nothing detracted from how wonderfully his sharp, defined features fit together. His jaw was strong and determined despite the boyish cleft in his chin. His lips, though set in a straight line of resolve, were full—and Skye recalled all too well how exciting it had felt to kiss him last night, despite all that was going on around them.

"Too bad we didn't get Marinaro the night he shot Danver and me," Trevor said. "It would have saved that lady from one hell of a bad situation. Not to mention the vic who died."

"No sense going backward," Skye said. "Before I left the station, I checked with some of the detectives to see if there were any more Marinaro sightings or tips. They said there were the usual calls from good citizens who want to help after an ugly incident, but so far none has resulted in anything helpful."

"Which is where you come in." Trevor waited as the male, informally dressed server refilled their wine from the bottle and whisked away their nearly empty salad dishes.

"How can Bella and I help?" Skye asked, leaning toward him when the server had gone. "No one, not even the department's best, seems to have a clue."

"I've got some ideas," Trevor said. "The thing is, I won't have as much time as I'd like to deal with him until I can put my other commitments behind me."

He paused while Skye was served a luscious-looking grilled halibut steak, and the thresher shark teriyaki that Trevor had ordered was placed in front of him. The aromas of the freshly cooked seafood dishes made Skye's mouth water, and she picked up her fork, ready to dig in.

After a few bites, Trevor said, "Try some of this." He cut off a little of his fish and passed it onto Skye's plate. She did the same—and found the gesture oddly but pleasurably intimate.

"Anyway," Trevor continued, "I'm sure you can appreciate why it's personal with me." He speared a bit of his shark and thrust it into his mouth. Skye watched as his lips closed and he chewed fiercely, as if he was as much of a predator as the food he ate. Perhaps he was, in his drive to capture Marinaro.

"Of course I understand," she said. "But I don't see how—"

"I'll have an edge if I can work with Bella and you. Your dog seems smart, and good at what she does."

"She sure is," Skye acknowledged.

"Above all, she's gotten Marinaro's scent, and not just once but twice. I've a few ideas where to search for him, and once I get some confirmation I want Bella, and you, to help nail him at one of those locations. Can I count on you?"

"You're talking about doing this while we're off duty," Skye hedged. "Unofficially." She suspected he did a lot of things unofficially if he thought it would help bring down the bad guys. She wasn't necessarily against it, but needed all the facts about what she was getting into.

"Yes. That means we'll have to rely a lot on each other. If things go down wrong, we could both get into trouble."

"I understand, but I reserve the right to opt out at any time."

"Got it," he said.

He was being awfully nice. Conciliatory. And damned sexy, with his heavy-lidded, attentive smile.

"I guess we have a deal," she said. "And if I hear of any leads on finding the suspect, I'll keep you informed. But—well, I'm curious. How did you happen to become a cop in the first place?"

His expression suddenly grew studiously blank again. "I was a naive kid when I decided that's what I'd do. I had the odd notion I could make sure justice always triumphed."

"I get it." And she did, kind of. She didn't condone what she had found in his files, but she assumed he had been looking for justice in his own way—and that way had gone awry with those terrible suspects, who'd attacked him.

Or was she being naive, too?

"No, I don't think you do get it," he contradicted. "Since I'm asking for your help, I guess it's fair that you understand what's driving me. The thing is, ever since I was a kid, I knew that justice doesn't often—or even usually—triumph, so I try to even the odds."

"What do you mean?" He looked tense and angry, so Skye reached across the table and gently touched his arm. It felt as if he'd tautened every muscle into tempered metal.

He stared at her. "Long story short? When I was a kid, my dad owned a convenience store. Some punks came in one day, robbed and shot him. Turned out they'd done it before. The evidence against them in the earlier case had supposedly seemed incontrovertible—till they got put on trial. Usual story—they got off on a technicality. They weren't nabbed after my dad's death and they killed again before they were finally caught. They wound up being convicted, but it was too late for my dad and the others. That's what sent me into law enforcement. And now I do everything I can—*everything*—to help the good guys win and stop killers before they harm more civilians. Now, you want out before we start?"

His hand suddenly grasped hers so tightly it almost hurt. His dark eyes bored into hers challengingly. Fiercely.

They sparked something way down inside her.

She wanted to hold the little boy he'd been. And she wanted to help tame the furious beast that now dwelled deep inside his soul, crying out for help. For justice.

"No, I'm in, Trevor, she said softly. "Just tell me what you want me to do."

Trevor never meant to bring up that stuff about his father. But Skye was really something. Something nice, which was a real turn-on.

Everything about her was a turn-on. In fact, as much as he needed to recruit her help in his scheme to track down Marinaro, he also just wanted to tear off her clothes and take her.

For now, though, he was just going to concentrate on staying with her for as long as he could.

The young, eager server who seemed to be bucking for a large tip came to the table to see if they wanted coffee.

"Sure. Black. How about you?" he asked Skye.

"Coffee sounds good." The server trotted off. "Actually I'm already feeling kind of jumpy. I don't think I'll sleep well tonight, and coffee won't help."

I know what would help you sleep, Trevor thought.

The pupils of her brilliant blue eyes widened as if she heard what he was thinking. Well, hell, she didn't have to hear his thoughts to know what was on his mind. He was practically undressing her without even touching her.

"So how did you wind up in Angeles Beach?" he asked, as if the question had been on the tip of his tongue all night. In a way, it had. He wanted to know about her. *Everything* about her.

"I chose it over a lot of other possible locations," she responded. "Not just me, but also some friends from childhood. Ron Gollar, of course, and two female buddies. We decided to stick together, so we looked for a place with opportunities for all of us. I'd taken basic training at a police academy near where I grew up. Then, after spending a few years on a police force, I trained as a K-9 cop. My girlfriends were both in the health care profession. Angeles Beach seemed perfect, especially when a spot opened up for a K-9 officer. Ron went into the military but decided to join us when he got out."

"Where'd you grow up?"

The server came by with their coffee, and she took a sip. "Minnesota."

"Ice country," Trevor said. "No wonder you ended up here. It's a lot warmer in Southern California."

"True," she said. "I don't necessarily mind the cold, but, well, this just turned out to be a place we could all agree on."

So why did those gorgeous blue eyes of hers turn so shifty? She usually seemed so up front, so in-your-face, boring into him with her gaze as if attempting to figure out everything he was thinking. But not now. Was there something she was hiding? He planned on finding out.

"So all of you came here to big, bad California. What did your families think about that?"

"They weren't happy about it," Skye said, "but what parents like their kids to move far away?" Her tone had grown firm again, her expression hardened, and Trevor figured he'd hit a sore spot. If only he understood what it was, and why it bothered her so much.

Much too soon, they'd both finished their coffees. Time to drive Skye home. At least he'd get to stay in her company for a little while longer.

The Angeles Beach streets on the way to her home were remarkably empty. Soon, they pulled up to the door of the house she shared with Bella. He parked at the curb and went around to do the gentlemanly thing and open her door, but she was already out of the car.

"I enjoyed tonight a lot, Trevor," Skye said. "Please let me know how Bella and I can help find Marinaro. And, well, would you like to come in for a little while to talk about it?"

She'd started out by avoiding his gaze as she stood

beneath the white glare of the streetlight overhead. But now she was looking right at him. Her mouth was open just a little, as if inviting him to kiss it. Hard. Heatedly.

"I'd like that a lot." He used the remote on his key chain to lock his car and grabbed her hand as they hurried up the walk.

As soon as they got inside, Trevor took Skye into his arms. But of course they were greeted by Bella, who barked insistently.

"She needs to go out." Skye sounded apologetic as she put the dog on a leash and left Trevor sitting on her living room couch—waiting, thinking, anticipating.

Chapter 13

As soon as she came back in, Trevor pulled her against him, and his mouth claimed hers.

Bad idea! Bad idea! The words reverberated in Skye's brain.

But there was no stopping now. He pushed his hard, hard body against her. His mouth was fiery, and his tongue engaged hers in sensually teasing games.

"This way," she somehow murmured against him, pushing him backward down the hallway toward her bedroom, her breasts against his chest.

Good thing Bella knew Trevor. Skye was aware of

her dog's keeping pace with them, uneasily pattering down the hall, watching how they suddenly seemed fused together—a single, burning human being instead of two cool cops.

Cops. They were coworkers.

Bad idea.

Her house suddenly seemed very, very full. And hot. She didn't have air-conditioning because it was so close to the beach, but right now she felt as if it burned with flames stoked by Santa Ana winds.

No, that was just her burning.

She was aware, so aware, of how Trevor's hands stroked her over her flimsy silk dress. Her back. Her butt. "Oh," she gasped.

And Bella barked.

"I'm fine, girl," Skye managed to say, smiling despite herself. Trevor and she had reached her bedroom. Her K-9 companion might be mostly trained to follow scents, but she was protective, too. "Down," Skye ordered her. "Stay."

She'd barely shut the door behind Trevor and her when he started undoing the buttons at the front of her dress.

Feeling vulnerable and wanting to participate, Skye ripped at Trevor's shirt. Its buttons popped open, revealing his hard, muscular chest, a hint of dark hair at its center. She ran her hands along it, then down toward his belt buckle.

"Wait!" he commanded, then threw off his shirt and undid his own pants, shoving them to the floor along with his boxers.

His scent was that of antiperspirant soap mixed with the pure, musky aroma of man. His skin was rough, hairy—all masculine.

He growled something, pulled her close but not against him, and in moments she, too, was bare.

And on the bed. With him. His hands, his mouth, they were everywhere. She wanted to give as good as she got, only she found herself gasping for more. And more.

He stopped for only a moment, and she heard the sound of wrapping being torn from a condom. The guy was always prepared.

His hand was back between her legs. Caressing her even as she bucked. "Now!" she exclaimed. "Please!"

Moments later, he complied with her command. He was inside her, thrusting, as she encouraged and moved with him, in unison.

She gasped loudly as her quick, hard climax overwhelmed her. A shout told her that he, too, had reached the pinnacle.

She clasped him tightly, breathing so heavily

that she wondered if she would lose consciousness. But she didn't want to miss even an instant of this insane pleasure, even when the best was over…for the moment.

"You okay?" he asked breathlessly a minute later.

"Oh, yeah," she said. "You?"

"Oh, yeah," he echoed.

As they continued to lie there, Skye's conscience once again began to berate her, but she pushed those thoughts aside.

This might have been a bad idea, but she wouldn't have missed it for anything—no matter what the consequences.

"You can't stay for the rest of the night?" Skye's voice sounded both exhausted and a little hurt. A pang of conscience shot through Trevor, but as wonderful as this had been and as much as he didn't want it to end, there was something he had to do.

"I'll take a rain check." He leaned over to kiss Skye on her sexy, swollen lips as her head lay on her pillow and her long blond hair spread out in delicious waves surrounding her head.

He was tempted to stay but drew himself up and dragged himself out of bed.

"Okay if I take a shower?" he asked.

"Help yourself," she said coolly.

"I wish I could stay, Skye, but duty calls." He responded to the question he saw in her eyes. "Nothing official, but there's someplace I have to go right now. And, well, this has been… I mean, I'd really like to do it again, and—"

"I got it," she finally said with a brief laugh. "Now get ready and get out of here. But let Bella into the bedroom when you head for the shower."

Skye snuggled into her soft and rumpled sheets, still breathing the scent of their lovemaking—letting it surround her with the memory of delight and the anticipation of more to come.

But she felt certain that, in the harsh light of day—when she raised her sore yet satisfied body from bed, when the glow of lovemaking wore off as she started getting ready for work, and the hurt that he hadn't stayed the night overpowered the remembered pleasure—she would know better.

The first glimmer of daylight appeared behind her closed draperies. On the floor beside her, Bella stirred, then stood, turning in a circle that signified that the beautiful black Malinois was ready to face the day and had to go outside to start it her usual way.

The action made Skye feel the impending day was going to be normal—mundane.

"That's good," Skye said aloud, softly.

But she knew she lied to herself. This day wouldn't be normal at all. Not with the memories of last night at the forefront of her mind and tingling along every inch of her skin.

No, today was going to be different. She just knew it.

Could it really be this easy?

In the pale light of daybreak, Trevor watched as a dark, stooped figure sneaked through the shrubbery behind the ocean-view mansion. The owner's business manager owed Trevor a favor and had promised to leave the doors open for him.

The owner was out of town. And Trevor had made sure to say the place was empty when he called a certain company requesting an estimate for a major landscaping upgrade. He mentioned, however, that a real estate broker might stop over that morning to do an initial walk-through for a possible sale.

All lies. All designed to set the trap Trevor had been planning for a while.

He had work to do and hoped he'd be able to accomplish it outside. Trevor didn't want to ruin any part of the decor of this beautiful house. Blood spatter tended to do that. But if inside was the only way…well, so be it. He'd just have to see how this played out.

Just then the figure darted out of Trevor's view, probably nearing the back door. Showtime.

"Good morning, Eddy." Trevor left the cover of shadows and approached his prey.

Sure enough, Edinger, dressed in baggy black sweats, was on the back porch. He froze like the proverbial deer caught in headlights. But he was no stately wild stag in search of a dinner of fine foliage.

No, his affinity for greenery had to do with stealing cash from people's homes or their persons.

"What the hell do you want, Owens?" In the pale light of dawn, Edinger looked even more rodentlike, with his large nose and buck teeth and pale skin. His hands were suddenly shoved into his pockets, and he slumped with his back against the beige stucco wall of the house.

Trevor put his own hands out in a gesture intended to appear placating. He didn't really want to soothe this rat, though.

"I'm just keeping an eye on you, like I promised," Trevor said with a big smile. "And what are you doing here?"

"How'd you know I'd be here?"

"I just guessed—after calling the company you work for. I told them all about how this house is going on the market and the real estate agent is hanging around, plus the place needs some landscaping while the owner's out of town. Isn't that the kind of setup you like best?"

"Hey, I was found not guilty." The jerk actually sounded indignant, and he straightened himself as he scowled.

"That doesn't mean anyone believes you're innocent," Trevor said menacingly. "We both know better, don't we, Eddy?"

"Look, cop, just leave me alone. I know my rights. Like I told you on the phone, you're harassing me. Maybe stalking me. I really will sue you and the whole police department for what you're doing if you don't stop."

"Gee, Eddy, that would be a civil action. Not that you'd win, of course. But by the time the lawyers talked, and the thing got to court…well, you and I would have seen a whole lot of each other before anything could happen." This wasn't entirely true, of course. Eddy's lawyers would know all about temporary restraining orders, things that could happen a lot faster than waiting for a claim to get to trial. But Eddy didn't necessarily know that.

"Leave me alone, you son of a bitch." Eddy lunged toward Trevor. A knife with one hell of a long, sharp-looking blade was in his hand.

Trevor moved, but not far enough away to ensure that he wasn't stabbed at all. He dodged just enough to let the knife get him in the left side. He purposely hadn't worn any Kevlar protection.

"Okay, you son of a bitch," Trevor growled, grabbing the small semiautomatic holstered under his loose shirt. He held it with both hands and momentarily pointed it at the ground. Furiously, he looked Eddy in the eye. "You're not going to hurt anyone else. Ever. You die. Right now. You hear me? Die."

He raised the gun and aimed it at Eddy—only to see, to his utter astonishment, that the guy clutched his chest and gasped. His eyes widened, like he was in pain. "You...you..." he whispered, as he crumpled to the ground in a heap.

Trevor blinked. Daylight was growing brighter, but he couldn't see any telltale rise and fall of the guy's chest.

Even so, he kept his gun trained on Edinger. "Eddy? Hey, Eddy, you okay?" It was a dumb thing to ask considering that he'd intended to shoot the guy and kill him in self-defense.

Eddy didn't respond. Didn't move. Carefully,

slowly, Trevor knelt, ignoring the pain in his side and the streaming of his blood down his shirt and pant leg. He remained ready to spring up and protect himself when Eddy stopped his pretense and attacked.

Only, Eddy remained still. And, touching his neck, Trevor felt no pulse.

Had he had a heart attack? Died out of fear that Trevor was about to kill him?

How ridiculous! But what other explanation could there be?

Trevor stood again, still moving slowly and painfully, then drew his cell phone from his pocket. He called 911. "This is Officer Trevor Owens of the ABPD. I need assistance." He gave the address. "Send the EMTs. I've been wounded, and I've got a suspect down."

Only…he hadn't done a damned thing to put him there.

What the hell had just happened here?

Chapter 14

Skye was heading for the station when she heard the call on her radio: "Officer down."

Oh, no, not another one, she thought. *Who is it?*

Not Trevor. Surely it couldn't be him.

The report seemed garbled. No shooting, but still a possible fatality. The dispatcher didn't have the full story—or wasn't reporting it.

There were lots of other officers in the ABPD. It could just as likely be her dear friend, Ron Gollar.

Skye shivered. She hated the idea that it was probably someone she knew.

She tried calling Trevor on his cell. No answer. That worried her.

At least Ron answered his phone. "I heard, Skye. I'm fine. But I don't have any details."

She called the station. The watch commander, a blasé old sergeant named Hutchings, didn't know the details, either. All he could tell her was that Trevor was wounded off duty and was being taken by ambulance to Angeles Beach Medical Center.

Skye's pulse rate skyrocketed, and she pulled cautiously to the side of the road. She needed a moment to let her suddenly fried mind compute the best way to the hospital. Fast.

"No K-9s were called in, Rydell," the commander continued. "The suspect was fatally injured. He appeared to be acting alone, so we don't need any tracking."

Good thing. Skye didn't want any distractions. She needed to get to the hospital and check on Trevor's condition.

What if he was dying...again? Once again she wondered if she could save him a second time. No one, as she was growing up, had ever addressed that possibility. She didn't know if anyone with her heritage had even tried such a thing, let alone succeeded.

"Good to know, sir," Skye said, "since I'll be a

little late reporting for duty today." She didn't try to explain or come up with some lame excuse.

After hanging up, she breathed deeply with her head touching the steering wheel. Behind her, sensing something wrong, Bella barked.

"I'm okay, girl," Skye assured her, hoping it was true. She didn't want to take the time to drive Bella home. She'd have to leave her in the car for at least a short while when they reached the hospital. Worst case, she'd call another K-9 officer to bring her to the station until Skye got there.

She was about two miles from the medical center and thought about using lights and sirens to keep everyone out of her way. But she didn't want to attract that kind of attention.

Yet what if Trevor was mortally wounded? Time was absolutely of the essence even though she heard no chanting inside her mind—at least not yet.

She ignored the speed limit but didn't resort to using official gear to get through the light traffic. The hospital had an indoor parking garage, and Skye dashed inside, pulled into a space near the emergency entrance and lowered the windows enough to give Bella some ventilation.

"I'll be back as soon as I can," she told her partner, giving her a brief hug before locking the doors.

She hurried into the emergency room. At the entrance was a row of desks where patients, or their families, signed in and showed insurance cards, and beyond was a room filled with people waiting either for a doctor or for their loved ones. The place smelled of antiseptic and fear.

Skye brushed her own fear aside and spoke with the admissions nurse. "A police officer was brought in a little while ago. Where—"

The nurse pointed beyond the waiting room. "Third room down the hall. But he's not alone. Would you like for me to—"

Skye did not wait to hear her question, but hurried through the waiting room. She heard voices from beyond the door. Should she knock? Maybe he was being examined by the doctors. Or—

The hell with waiting. She gave a brief knock and walked in before anyone responded.

And found Trevor there, lying in bed, surrounded not by doctors but by Captain Boyd Franks and SWAT officers Carl Shavinsky and Greg Blanding.

Trevor was sitting up and looked alert as he stared right at her and gave a lopsided smile that made her heart do flip-flops.

But it also called attention to her. The others turned toward the door, where she stood.

"Oh, excuse me," she said. "I was close by and wanted to make sure there wasn't anything I could do to help, and—"

"Everything's under control, Officer Rydell," Captain Franks said coolly.

"But thanks for checking," Trevor said. "I'll be out in an hour or two. Fortunately, I wasn't hurt bad, but you should have seen the other guy."

His tone suggested he was joking. And his gaze told her he remembered last night. She felt herself blush, hoping the others wouldn't understand why. She straightened her shoulders, trying to be all business. She looked into Trevor's eyes. Whatever his injury was, it apparently wasn't life threatening. He appeared almost, well, pleased. But as he looked back at her, she sensed something else, too. Confusion?

What was going on?

"Could you just tell me briefly what happened so I can tell the others who ask? If that's all right, sir," Skye asked, looking from Trevor to the captain.

"It's okay to let everyone know that Officer Owens was injured but will be fine," Captain Franks said.

"Can I say how he was hurt?"

The captain nodded at Trevor, obviously giving him permission to explain.

"Damnedest thing," Trevor said. "I'd been keeping an eye on Edinger. I figured it was unlikely he'd act again so soon after his acquittal, but he obviously was unstable enough to murder that broker and home owner in the first place. I thought I was being fairly discreet."

Something about his expression told her otherwise. He seemed like a small child crossing his fingers behind his back while telling his parents a whopper.

"But he saw me. Came at me with a knife. Got me in the side." He gingerly reached down beneath the white blanket and winced as he touched somewhere below his rib cage. "Of course I'd come armed, since I didn't trust the guy. I was prepared to draw my weapon to protect myself, in self-defense."

So that was it. Another incident like those in which Trevor had killed murder suspects who had gotten off at trial—purportedly in self-defense. And maybe actually so. But Skye suspected he had pushed and pushed the suspects until they erupted and attacked. That way he could shoot back—attain his own form of justice.

He continued. "In the heat of the moment, before I finished drawing and aiming my gun, I shouted at him to die. Right away. Dumb thing to do, but...well, I don't know if he had a heart condition or what, but he just dropped. Right there, in front of me. When I checked, I felt no pulse. It's like when I told him to die, that's exactly what he did."

Skye swallowed her gasp. Could that line of legends from her heritage be true?

He was the one who'd been wounded, but Trevor watched as Skye's face grew as white as if she'd just been stabbed. At the same time she edged toward the door, obviously not wanting anyone to notice her distress.

He wouldn't call attention to her reaction to the others, who watched him, nodding and whispering among themselves. He'd let her exit gracefully.

But when he was out of here, he would get together with her as soon as possible. Find out what she was thinking.

Carl Shavinsky followed his gaze and started to turn toward Skye. To divert him, Trevor said, "Hey, guys, how do you want to handle this with the media? I mean, I assume someone out there will want my side of what happened."

"We'll get the media liaisons at the station to talk to you first," the captain said, which started a lively conversation about what slimeballs reporters could be.

But it didn't completely take Trevor's attention off Skye.

"You okay, Skye?" Greg Blanding looked over Shavinsky's shoulder toward the door.

"Absolutely," she said as she opened it, "but I have to check on Bella. I left her in my car. I'll let everyone know Trevor's okay. They'll all be as glad as me."

She didn't look glad. Maybe she was just trying to hide any indication of all they'd shared last night, but he thought it was more than that.

She appeared to have gotten herself together, though. The color was returning to her cheeks, and her beautiful face was as expressionless as if she'd wiped all emotion out of her system.

But he knew better.

"Thanks for coming to check on me, Skye," he said. "See you at the station."

Not only there, of course. He still wanted her assistance in finding Marinaro.

And most of all, he'd like to visit her at home. Again. Soon.

The back patio at Skye's home wasn't large, but it easily accommodated four people. Once again, she had contacted her longtime friends for an evening get-together. This time Ron had been delegated the duty of bringing pizza.

They all sat on molded plastic chairs around a

glass table with an umbrella in the center, sipping on light beer and nibbling the remnants of the thin-crust pepperoni pizza.

Like the last time they had been together, twilight was just beginning to fall on this warm summer evening.

Beyond the patio, in the small, grassy yard surrounded by a tall wooden fence, Bella romped with Hayley's dog, a gray midsized terrier mix she had adopted from a shelter two years earlier. His name was Frenzy, since he always seemed full of energy. The dogs were arguing amiably over a large plastic bone, and each barked as the other took it away.

"Okay, spit it out, already," Kara blurted, looking at Skye. She put her glass down and stood, her hands on her curvy hips. Her long black hair fanned out around her shoulders. "You called us all, said something unnerving happened and you needed to talk about it. But every time we've brought it up this evening, you keep saying you need to get your thoughts together before you explain."

"Right. I say you've had plenty of time to get those thoughts together." Hayley also rose and crossed her arms over her chest. She was casually clad, in denim shorts and a plain pink T-shirt.

Only Ron remained seated with Skye. He'd

brought along some beer, although only Skye had taken him up on a bottle. "She'll tell us when she's ready." He took a swig of the amber brew, but his light blue eyes reflected concern. "Ah, hell." He stood like the others, pulling at the edges of his white Angeles Beach T-shirt. "I'm as curious as they are. What's up, Rydell?"

"Sit down, please. All of you." Skye gestured toward the empty seats and strengthened her courage by taking a swig of the cold beer. "When you were being taught about our hereditary abilities, did you ever hear the legend of how some of our powers might be passed along to people we saved?"

"It's just a story, Skye." Ron shook his head as he lowered himself obediently onto his seat. "When you were learning how to use these abilities, I spent a lot of time studying up on them, just because I was interested and because my mother had them, too. You know that."

Skye nodded. In fact, she'd suspected that Ron, like other males among their peers, was a little jealous of their gift, although he was never too obvious about it.

"There were a lot of legends to learn," he continued, "though most were interesting. I liked the ones about the afterlife, especially the one about how those people you help over the rainbow bridge go to a modern version of Valhalla, where they share a really great eternity with our ancestresses."

Skye liked that account, too, and really hoped that, of all the legends, it was true. It provided such a wonderful rationale for them to exercise their powers. The three friends had often discussed whom they heard chanting and what the foreign-sounding words meant, but they had no answers, and neither did their mothers. But they knew, of course, that women like them did good. When appropriate, those with their powers made immediate decisions that brought people back from certain death. That was the best part.

"Some legends have apparent bases in truth," Ron was saying. "Hard to know the difference. Sometimes, Valkyrie powers were said to run amok. A few cases resulted in the rescued person's accidentally acquiring Valkyrie abilities in reverse—the ability to take, not save, lives. The most unsavory took advantage, killing their adversaries with it."

"I never heard about it quite that way," Kara said. "What my mother told me was much more...well, romantic, I guess."

"If you call gaining an ability to kill people romantic," Hayley said dryly. And then she stopped. And stared at Skye. "Are you telling us that the cop you saved actually has that power now? We were always told it was strictly an old wives' tale."

"An old Valkyrie wives' tale," Kara corrected. She, too, seemed to watch Skye's face for her reaction.

Skye felt herself redden. "Look, I don't really know what happened. I wasn't there. But there was an incident early this morning. Do you remember hearing about the murder trial of a guy called Eddy Edinger?"

"The SOB of a killer got off on a technicality," Ron said, again gulping some beer.

"Exactly." Skye paused to pat a panting Bella, who'd just run onto the porch. Frenzy followed, stopping at the bowl of water Skye had left near the kitchen door. As Bella, too, went after a drink, Skye described what she had heard about that morning's incident. "Officer Trevor Owens, the SWAT guy I kept from dying a few weeks ago, was off duty, but he was there. The suspect apparently stabbed him in the side with a knife. Officer Owens pulled a gun and aimed it, while at the same time—or so he said—he told the suspect to die, right then and there. He said he was just yelling the command in the heat of the moment. He didn't expect it to happen, figured Edinger must have been scared when he drew his weapon. Maybe he had a medical condition. Who knows? But the fact was, he died. Right then and there."

Her friends stayed silent for a long, unnerving moment. Skye knew where their thoughts were going. Well, heck, let them guess. She couldn't exactly hide it...could she?

"Okay, honey." Hayley's face was solemn but her pale blue eyes were twinkling irritatingly. "How well have you gotten to know Officer Owens?"

Skye stood abruptly, her chair scraping noisily along the patio's cement. "Cut it out!" she shouted. Then, realizing her neighbors might hear, she quieted down. "Like I told you all before, I don't understand why I felt I had to save Trevor. But the one thing I do know is that the sexual attraction between us is, well, amazing. And, yeah, don't you dare give me a hard time, but we made love last night. Then he left, and that thing occurred where Edinger died."

Ron took a sip of his beer and then smirked. "You're saying that the version you heard was...what? If one of you saves the life of some guy and then has sex with him, he's somehow charged with your abilities?"

"Well, Ron, there's more to it than that," Hayley said. "At least the way I understand it. It can't just be any guy, but one who also has some Nordic heritage. But, yes, there has to be some kind of connection with the Valkyrie descendant who saves him. Sexual, at least, and maybe more."

"Awesome!" Ron exclaimed. "So all I need to do is go back to Minnesota, get my ass saved by one of the ladies with powers like yours—someone I don't know as well as any of you, of course, or I couldn't stand it. Then take her to bed, and I'll be just like you? Well, what do you know!" His grin was huge. "Hey, talk about friends with benefits. A little fun, a little justice—"

"Not funny, Ron," Skye said glumly, although she suspected he wasn't entirely joking. "The thing is, if this is true, then I have some responsibility for Edinger's death." She held up her hand as the others' mouths all opened, as if they prepared to protest. "I know what an awful scumbag he was. If the evidence against him was true, he killed two people for no reason. Maybe more, in other similar incidents. But our legal system, rightly or wrongly, held him not guilty despite the evidence."

"He also stabbed your buddy Trevor," Kara reminded her, standing and putting her hands on Skye's shoulders. "He might have killed him instead. And you said Trevor grabbed his own gun. Whichever way he killed the guy, it was self-defense."

"That's true," Hayley agreed with a nod.

Daylight had been fading without Skye's noticing it, and now they were nearly sitting in the dark.

"You're all correct," she conceded. "And it wasn't as if I chose to kill the guy, whether or not he deserved it. And he did—this time. But our mandate, from the time we realized we had some choices over who would live, was to help people, not kill those who weren't already dying."

She rose and walked to her back door, flipping the switch to illuminate the porch with lights attached to her house.

"*Good* people," Hayley reminded her. "We're supposed to sense who deserves our help and either save them, if possible, or see them to a peaceful afterlife."

Skye turned again to her friends, who were all watching her with obvious concern. "How would you feel if you were in this position?" she asked. "If you might have somehow given another powers that were potentially harmful to people. If that's what's happened with Trevor, what if he uses these powers again—maybe even to kill someone who isn't a creep like Edinger? His standards of who deserves to live, and who doesn't, could be a lot different from ours. What if he kills someone we wouldn't want harmed, for whatever reason?"

"Good point." Kara nodded.

"Looks like you ladies had better watch who you

save…and take to bed. In any event, here's to Owens and his stopping that bastard Edinger. The world needs more good guys like him." Ron, lifting his beer bottle, took a last swig from it and frowned. "Hey, I'm going in for another one. Or two. Anybody else need something from the kitchen?" As he neared Skye at the doorway, he gave her a hug. "Don't sweat it, Rydell. You didn't do anything wrong. And I hope you had a damned good time doing it!" He winked, then pushed open the door. The dogs followed him, obviously hoping for a treat.

"There are times," Hayley said, watching him from the table, "that I'd love to kick our friend Gollar in his butt—which is apparently the location of his puny brain."

Skye laughed with her friends, but stopped when Kara asked, "Is there really something between Trevor and you, Skye? I mean more than sex. Something special?"

Skye started to nod, then stopped herself. "I think so, but honestly, I don't understand it. I'd barely noticed the guy before that day at the warehouse, and yet all of a sudden I felt some weird compulsion to save his life. Are we connected? Is he the love of my life?"

"What are you going to do now?" Hayley asked.

"Hell if I know." Skye tossed her hands up in a

gesture of frustration. "I'll have to play it by ear, I guess. But if Trevor actually got that power from me, do I have to purposefully do something to retrieve it? If so, what do I have to do?"

Secretly, she wondered what would happen if she got the power back. Would that mean she'd have to stay away from him to ensure that he didn't get it again?

The very idea seemed to puncture Skye's soul.

Chapter 15

Trevor stood in the corridor on the station's sixth floor, where the top brass hung out. The door to the favorite conference room of the Force Investigation Division was closed, and he'd been told to wait in the quiet, sterile-looking hall till the captain came out for him.

Too bad he wouldn't see Skye here, as he had last time. She'd had some involvement in that situation, but not this one.

He wanted to talk to her, though. *Really* wanted to talk to her. The time they'd spent together before he'd gone to confront Eddy—well, that had occupied his mind every waking minute since. And his dreams during his brief doses of sleep.

But she had avoided him all weekend, and he didn't know why. He'd find out what was up with her, though. Today. Even if she didn't return his calls, she would come to work, and he was already here despite the fact that he'd been placed on temporary leave. He'd see her. She'd see him. And he'd get an explanation.

It was Monday morning, and he was in uniform. He had been called in to give a statement and answer questions about the incident with Eddy.

The door opened. "Come in, Officer Owens," said Captain Boyd Franks.

Trevor left his attitude in the hall, as always. Though he'd done nothing wrong—especially this time—being respectful was the best way to keep his job. And he liked his job. A lot.

The usual suspects sat at the table: the director of the FID, Lieutenant Theresa Agnew; and its civilian representative, John Correy. As with the last time, it was a pared-down group of investigators, since Trevor hadn't fired his weapon.

Trevor took his regular seat at the head of the table, wishing they'd replace it with something more comfortable than these wooden chairs. Maybe the idea was to ensure that those who sat there got sore butts.

"So, Officer Owens," Lieutenant Agnew began, "this is becoming a standing appointment, I'm afraid." She sat directly to his right. At least there was a smile on her pinched face, and Trevor smiled back, briefly.

"Yes, ma'am," he said. "After getting shot, and now stabbed, I'm beginning to feel like one of those voodoo dolls that always gets punctured." He wanted to remind them right off that he'd been injured again.

"But you're all right, aren't you?" Correy asked. He wore a gray suit this time and sat beyond Captain Franks on Trevor's other side. He actually looked concerned. Nice guy. Maybe.

"Yes, sir."

"But Eddy Edinger isn't," Agnew reminded them unnecessarily. "We're here to get your interpretation of the events that led to his death."

Trevor nodded, then asked, "Is the coroner's report out yet?"

"Only a preliminary one." The captain shook his head slowly. "Cause of death is listed, for now, as cardiac arrest, for reasons unknown. His autopsy isn't complete yet, though."

"I see." But Trevor didn't—not really. He'd seen no indication that the guy was sick. He'd also read the media reports, and lots of questions were being asked. Apparently, Eddy had seemed entirely healthy during his trial. And he didn't seem the type to get freaked out if a gun was aimed at him.

Even so, the louse was dead, and Trevor hadn't used any weapon on him.

At the captain's urging, Trevor told his version of what had happened. How Eddy had surprised him— sort of—and come at him with a knife. How he'd been wounded, but not seriously, and in self-defense, he'd reached for his weapon while telling the SOB to back off.

Of course what he'd really done was to tell the guy to die, but there weren't any witnesses, and that would sound weird here, wouldn't it?

"That's all you did?" John Correy asked when he was done.

Okay, he had to be honest. "Well, I did sort of tell him that if he didn't back off, he was liable to die." Close enough.

"And what were you doing around that particular house at that hour of the morning?" Agnew asked.

Trevor had prepared himself for this one. It was the only thing that could hurt him in this investigation.

"The owner's Marlon Manfredy." They all nodded at the name of one of Hollywood's biggest movers and shakers. "I know his business manager. Mr. Manfredy travels a lot, and he's really concerned about security. I've been conducting an informal surveillance of the place while he's out of town. I'd awakened that night for no reason and decided I should go take a look there, like a hunch. I saw movement in the bushes, and there was Edinger."

"Did anything else bring you there?" Agnew asked. "Besides a hunch?"

Hell, Trevor would be skeptical, too, if he were in her position. But even if he'd been moonlighting in private security—which he hadn't—the department fortunately had no policy against it.

The captain came to his rescue, as he had done before in these sessions. "Does the reason really matter? Unless—" He turned to Trevor. "You didn't call Mr. Edinger and tell him to meet you there, or anything like that, did you?"

"No, sir," Trevor assured them. "I did call his landscaping company on the owner's behalf, but I didn't speak to Eddy." Which was true. His trap had been sprung indirectly. If Edinger hadn't heard from his landscaping company about the wealthy home owner being out of town, leaving his house ripe for a nice, lucrative burglary—and, potentially, a bonus murder or two if anyone like the real estate broker happened to show up—he wouldn't have been there that morning. No one had twisted his arm to go there.

"Okay, then," Captain Franks said. "I think we're through for now. The team that did the on-site investigation found nothing to contradict what you've said. We know where to find you if there are any further questions. Thank you, Officer Owens."

"You're welcome, sir." Trevor rose to leave, then paused. "You know, I'm really puzzled about Mr. Edinger's death, too," he said. "If the coroner's final report says anything different—"

"We'll be sure to let you know," said Franks.

Skye stared at her computer instead of working on her report of the crime scene she'd been at this morning. It would be a good report. Bella had performed perfectly—scenting an item that a victim said the robber had touched, then finding the suspect outside in the crowd of gawkers who were watching from behind the yellow tape. He'd tried to bolt, but Bella pounced, held him down and growled without hurting the guy. Now the suspect was in custody.

"Hey, Rydell," Manny Igoa called as he entered the room, his dog, Rusty, trotting beside his long legs. "I hear Bella and you are the heroes of the day." He stopped and patted her on the shoulder.

"Bella certainly is." Skye reached down to stroke behind the ears of her dog, who was now standing up and sniffing the latest K-9 to enter the room. "She's the one who found the guy."

"You're too modest." Manny sat down in his cubicle. "If you want to get somewhere around here, you need to sing your own praises. Or at least not give all the kudos to your dog. Bella will go as far in the department as you do, not vice versa."

"Could be."

"Hello, Skye. Igoa."

At the sound of Trevor's voice—sexy as hell despite its matter-of-fact tone—Skye startled and pressed an extra key on her computer. She quickly corrected the typo, which gave her a good excuse not to look at him while she gathered her fraying thoughts.

"Hi, Trevor," she said casually as Igoa, too, greeted him. "How are you feeling?"

He strode toward her, and it was all she could do not to grin sappily at him. No matter how he felt, he looked damned good in his SWAT uniform. He didn't seem to be in any pain as he stopped beside her and knelt to pat Bella's head. "If you're asking about my latest injury, heck, I already survived a bullet to the neck. A little stab in the ribs...that was nothing."

Igoa laughed. "Glad it was you instead of me."

Skye said nothing—not with Trevor's deep mahogany eyes boring into hers, as if her opinion about his being stabbed really mattered. Or maybe to question whether she could have somehow just looked at him and healed that stab wound instantly.

No. He might have suspicions, but he didn't really know about her.

But how could she avoid answering any questions he might have about her if she demanded the information from him that had been plaguing her—how had Eddy Edinger really died? She needed to know. Her conversations with her friends from home had only added to her unease. Sure, she had tried, all weekend, to convince herself that the old legends had no basis in truth.

Tried and failed.

She had to find out for sure.

She forced a smile—not hard to do with him so close. Her body stirred way deep down. She had a barely subdued urge to tear off his clothes and make love with him again.

As if.

"So," she said as casually as she could muster, "guess you're macho enough to survive anything. Not true for Edinger, though, I hear."

The suddenly grim expression on Trevor's handsome face made Skye want to reach out and comfort him. "Yeah. I'm surprised, but I feel sorry for the guy in a way. He just keeled over. It was like he literally got scared to death, or whatever, because I told him he was about to die...." He shook his head.

This was a confirmation from the source, Skye thought. But she still needed more information.

Impulsively she crooked her finger, motioning him to come closer. "I'm really glad you're okay," she said softly after he complied. She could smell his tangy scent of soap, shave cream and him, and it nearly drove her wild. But she couldn't give in to the attraction until she figured out what was really going on. "If you don't have any plans for dinner tonight, it'll be my treat."

She might have to violate her ancestors' insistence on utter secrecy about their abilities in order to learn how far any powers she might have inadvertently passed to Trevor went.

If the stories turned out to be true, she had to find a way to withdraw those abilities from Trevor—and she had a feeling he wouldn't like that.

Not at all.

"Thanks for inviting me, Skye." Standing at her door, Trevor thrust a bouquet of pink lilies and purple irises at her.

"They're beautiful!" she exclaimed, accepting

them and motioning him to come in. Oh, heavens, had this been even more of a mistake than she'd feared?

He'd taken her invitation as a romantic one. He made her glow all over—from lust and anticipation, as well as from embarrassment—when he bent down to kiss her, but she pulled away from him.

"Good to see you, Trevor," she said almost formally, glad she had worn a pretty but not particularly sexy gold button-front shirt that she'd tucked into brown slacks. "Come in."

Bella followed them down the hall to the kitchen, where Skye had prepared a simple meal of chicken Marsala over bow-tie pasta, with a salad on the side.

The lighting in her warm wood-and-tile kitchen, combined with the late-day glow of the sun, enriched the auburn highlights in Trevor's short brown hair. He'd worn a snug black T-shirt that hugged his amazingly muscular arms and chest, and jeans that also hid very little about his masculine physique. Skye's mouth watered—and not from the aroma of the dinner she had cooked.

She silently chastised herself. This man might have secret abilities that he didn't know about. She'd thought long and hard about how best to approach him about what had happened with Edinger.

"Looks delicious," he said as Skye handed him a

bowl to carry into the small adjoining dining room. It wasn't the food he looked at, though...but her.

She turned her head, so aware of the sensuality of the moment that even the touch of her own hair flowing around her shoulders heightened the desire she attempted to tamp down. "Um...I'm really hungry tonight," she said brightly, holding the plate of chicken as she swept past him into the dining room. "How about you?" And then she thought about the dual meaning that question could have and felt herself grow even hotter.

"Very." His deep, sexy tone made it clear that he, too, caught the ambiguity of what she'd asked.

"Why don't you sit there?" Skye pointed to a seat at the Early American–style wooden table. She'd set the table with wicker place mats, her everyday stainless flatware and usual dishes—nothing fancy. This wasn't an event to impress him.

But now she felt so flustered, so uncomfortable, that she wondered if she could even start the conversation without revealing too much. But she knew she had to talk with him. She couldn't let him keep thinking he was hallucinating when he thought she'd had something to do with his life being saved.

"Bella, down," she instructed as she took her own

seat. Bella obeyed, curling up on the edge of the red, navy and gold area rug beneath the table.

Skye served Chianti along with her version of the Italian dish. As they ate, she couldn't bring herself to ask detailed questions about the death of Edinger. She'd considered this before. So what if it wasn't an appetizing subject? They were both cops. They could talk about anything in a cool, professional manner.

Even so, they tiptoed around anything to do with their work. Skye found herself intrigued by which ball teams interested Trevor most—the L.A. Lakers and the San Diego Chargers. Angeles Beach wasn't quite large enough to support its own major teams, but Trevor was all for it happening someday. They talked about TV shows and movies and…well, everything except their jobs.

And Skye found herself not wanting to disturb the mood. But eventually they were done eating.

"Everything was delicious," Trevor said. "So you're a damned good K-9 cop and a great cook, too. Is there anything else I should know about you?"

A perfect opening. But just as Skye opened her mouth to ask about the Edinger incident, she found Trevor standing beside her. He pulled out her chair and she stood, as if it had been orchestrated in advance.

Suddenly—and not so unexpectedly—she was in

his arms, pressing against his hard body as his hot mouth explored hers and made everything inside her go liquid and limp.

"I've been waiting all night for dessert," Trevor whispered huskily against her mouth.

And without another thought for the real reason she'd invited him here, Skye led him down the hall once more, to her bedroom.

"Stay," she said hoarsely to Bella, then shut the door behind them.

Heaven wasn't supposed to be so hot, Skye thought as her clothes disappeared from her in barely more than an instant. Just as fast, she pulled off every stitch of clothing covering Trevor's outstandingly ripped body.

Immediately she saw the white bandage on his side, against his tanned skin.

She reached out, stroked it. "I'm so sorry," she said. "Does it hurt?"

"You could kiss it and make it better," he responded, his voice a sexy rasp.

She bent, kissed the bandage and brushed against the hardness of Trevor's erection...not entirely accidentally.

He groaned, and she took him into her mouth,

and they quickly wound up on her bed—making love with such abandon that Skye could think of absolutely nothing else but the amazing sensations everywhere on, and in, her body....

A while later, they lay beside each other in the tangle of her flowery sheets. Trevor's head was on her pillows, and hers was on his chest, enjoying its syncopated up-and-down motion as he tried to catch his breath.

"I'm so glad you're here," she blurted out. She was beginning to care for this man. A lot.

If only there weren't secrets between them.

"Me, too." He moved a little, and she was soon staring into his dark eyes. "I'm really falling for you, you know that?"

She hadn't known, but she'd hoped so. "Me, too," she said to him earnestly. "I really care a lot about you, Trevor. And that's why... Well, please tell me what happened between Edinger and you. Tell me exactly how he died."

He didn't really want to think about that now. Not after such stunning sex with Skye. He was falling in love with her. Dumb? Maybe. He didn't really know her that well. But it wasn't just sex that made him want to be with her.

He had wanted to get together with her over the weekend, but she had come up with one excuse after another. That had hurt.

Had she stayed away from him because of Edinger's death? If so, why?

Maybe he'd find out if he went along with her now and answered her questions.

And so, lying in bed, with her soft, fragrant hair tickling his chest, he held her to him tightly and told her how things had gone down.

How Eddy had simply…died. Well, maybe not so simply. He had stabbed Trevor. Trevor had threatened him. Told him the truth. He was going to die.

When he was done, Skye said, "That was why you didn't stay the night with me. You had an appointment with Edinger."

"Not an appointment, but he was on my radar and knew it."

"You were stalking him?"

"That's what he called it, not me."

"It was supposed to be like those other times, when you killed those suspects who got off murder charges at trial."

"Always in self-defense," he said firmly.

She laughed a little. "Always in set-up self-defense. And you got the Force Investigation guys to buy in to it. You may have saved some other lives in the process. But how did you feel when you killed them?"

Trevor felt her tense up, so he waited a minute, considering his answer. "I can't say I like killing people. But in those kinds of situations, it's more than revenge, if that's what you're thinking. I may be skirting the edge of what cops are allowed to do, but we're charged with saving lives, and that's what I'm doing. I'm preventing a few murderers who were released by an imperfect system from killing anyone else."

"Then you really don't like killing." It was a statement, not a question. "I'm glad to hear that. I... I'm going to tell you some things in strictest confidence, Trevor." She lifted her head, and he could read the earnestness in her gorgeous blue eyes. "Will you promise this will go no further? I have to reveal things I've vowed not to tell anyone, because I think you... I mean, I... Well, let's just say it may be very important that you understand who, and what, I am." Before he could voice his confusion, she continued. "I know I'm being cryptic, but I can't explain until I get your promise. Will you keep what I tell you to yourself?"

She was obviously very concerned. And very serious. And very beautiful. He couldn't refuse her anything just then, with her warm, naked body against his, her expression so confused and yet so caring....

"Scout's honor," he said with a smile, raising his hand as if taking an oath.

"SWAT's honor would be better."

He agreed.

"And there's another promise I need from you. With what I'm going to explain to you about Eddy Edinger, I need for you to swear that you're serious, that since you don't like killing, you won't use the…ability I'm about to describe, except as you've been doing without it—setting up suspects you're sure are guilty, I mean."

What the hell was she talking about?

"Yeah, right," he said, trying not to glare at her. "I promise." But what was she driving at?

He soon found out—and wished he hadn't. Skye told him an utterly bizarre and ridiculous story, sounding entirely serious.

It *was* ridiculous, wasn't it? Only…it would explain how he'd survived being shot in the neck by Marinaro and heard Skye calling him back to life. And why he'd had hallucinations of Wes Danver's death—and, nearly, his own. It would also explain what had happened to Edinger.

Would he tell anyone what Skye had said? Hell, no. He might back off really fast from the way he'd started to care for her, but he wouldn't be the instrument of her being tossed into a loony bin with the key thrown away.

When she was done, he extricated himself from her embrace and dressed quickly.

"You don't believe me," she said sadly. "I knew you wouldn't. At least not until you've had time to think about it and all that's happened. But you'll keep your promise, won't you?"

"Yeah, sure," he said.

Since they'd left the bedroom, Bella was back by her side. Skye had put on a soft white robe but was otherwise naked.

"And, yeah," he said, "in answer to your question, I do have some Scandinavian ancestors, on my maternal grandmother's side. I guess that's supposed to matter?"

"That's part of the legend," she affirmed.

"You have to admit," he retorted, "that it all sounds…well, crazy."

"That doesn't mean it isn't true." Her arms were crossed, and she looked both belligerent and defensive. "Look, Trevor. I know you don't buy it, but that's *your* problem. Mine is to make sure you don't abuse the power you think you don't have."

"Goodbye, Skye." He turned and strode out into the night.

Chapter 16

He thought she was nuts. No big surprise.

But it still hurt, Skye thought for at least the hundredth time since Trevor left a few hours ago. She got Bella out of her black-and-white in the station's parking lot that was lit with energy-saving outdoor lights.

Her partner and she were on the very early morning shift that day, and with luck, she wouldn't run into Trevor. Hopefully, his shift did not start until later.

Because they worked from the same location, she wouldn't be able to put off their meeting forever. In fact, that would be a bad idea. But she needed to steel herself against his scoffing...and keep close watch to make sure he didn't use his possible life-and-death power cavalierly.

Inside the station, she clocked in, and Bella and she headed for her cubicle. But before she got there, officers in full gear started streaming down the hall on either side of them. The radio on her utility belt sang out at the same time, giving the code number for her to report to a crime scene.

"Hey, you're here." Ron Gollar caught up with her. "Another shooting incident and possible homicide. Sounds like Marinaro's M.O. You called out on it?"

"I am now." Grimly, Skye confirmed with the chief, hurried with Bella to her locker to extract their protective gear and sped out.

The site was a strip mall in one of Angeles Beach's most seedy, unattractive areas. It was a popular spot for prostitution and drug dealing. Skye's initial thought was to wonder why the department's powers-that-be thought this was another of Marinaro's crimes. He hadn't worked under cover of darkness before. And a place like this wasn't his norm, either.

She parked her black-and-white and brought Bella out on her leash, donning her protective vest and helmet over her uniform and putting on Bella's gear. Standing with other newly arrived officers, Skye got

a rundown from the sergeant in charge of securing
the scene as she watched the EMTs hustle from their
vehicle and head to the alley behind a store, where
the victim had been found.

Although this was a commercial area, there were
apartment buildings nearby. A couple of residents
had apparently heard gunshots and called 911. When
a unit responded, they found a female victim in the
alleyway. Her clothes were ripped and she had apparently been sexually assaulted before being shot.
The injuries to her body and the location of the shots
were Marinaro-style.

When he was done, the sergeant hurried off. Skye
stood still for a moment, waiting. Listening—and
not just to the chaos of the crime scene around her.

But there was no chanting. No indication that the
victim hovered between life and death. Nothing Skye
could do for her. She was already gone.

She sighed, but didn't stand there for long. It was
time to do her other job: try to find who had done this.

Skye was given a shell casing and gloves dropped
at the scene for Bella to sniff, then search for the per-
petrator. She soon learned why the shopping center
was so popular with the less-than-savory crowd. It
was a rabbit warren of footpaths and alleyways and
passages that allowed quick getaways if the hookers

or dealers thought their shady transactions were compromised. This had to be another reason Marinaro was considered a suspect. His prior crime scenes also had easy means of escape.

The two K-9 officers on-site, Skye and Igoa, were paired with other cops for protection in this difficult area to monitor. Skye was relieved when Ron Gollar was assigned to accompany Bella and her. She trusted him to watch their backs.

"You girls lead the way," he told her, his weapon drawn.

As Skye let Bella determine where to go, she remained alert, keeping her partner close. Ron had to stay behind them, not what Skye preferred. Bella might be harmed before either Ron or she could reach the suspect. But the pathways between the one- and two-story buildings were narrow, and the dim illumination from her flashlight didn't let her see more than a few feet ahead.

Skye was almost relieved when Bella did not pick up a scent and acted confused. Even so, Skye quietly urged her to keep trying. Their footsteps were all she heard nearby, although the hum of voices around them kept her aware of all the activity at the scene.

Bella led them around another building before Skye turned to Ron. "I think our suspect got away."

"Any way for Bella to determine if it was really Marinaro?"

"I can compare her reaction to these items to the items left at scenes where we're sure he was the suspect. It won't convict him for this one, but it'll at least give us more reason to go after him—or not."

"Sounds good."

They headed back to the street, which was filled with black-and-whites, other officers and crime scene investigators. They met up with Ron's partner, Jim Herman, who had accompanied Manny Igoa and Rusty on a similar attempt to pick up the scent. Like Ron, Bella and her, they were still in full protective gear.

"Any luck?" Manny asked Skye, bending his long form to pat his partner's head.

"None," she said. "You?"

"No." Jim reached to remove his helmet. "But if our suspect's Marinaro, like it looks, his acts are escalating. He's killing women faster than before and getting less discriminating about his vics. By appearances, this lady's not a college girl or sweet young thing. We'll learn more once she's ID'd, but looks like she's a drug dealer and maybe a working girl, too."

"We can't just judge her by the area where she was found," Skye said, looking around again at their seedy environment.

"No, but one of the patrol officers who arrived first is assigned here often and thinks he recognized her," Jim said. "If so, she's been run in a time or two, charged but released."

"No matter what she was accused of, she didn't deserve this," Skye asserted.

She stopped talking. SWAT hadn't been called out. The situation involved no hostages or confining of dangerous suspects.

So why did she suddenly see Trevor standing on the street, talking to Captain Franks?

And why did she want to run up to him and have him hold her tight?

Trevor had seen Skye the moment he walked up to the site. The sag to her shoulders was due to more than the burden of her heavy protection equipment. Her dog hadn't located the suspect. The way Igoa looked, his hadn't, either.

The SOB had gotten away. Again.

Thanks to his conversation with the chief, Trevor felt certain Marinaro had struck once more.

"Yeah," Chief Franks was saying, "sure resembles

a familiar M.O. Could be a copycat, though." He looked even older than usual. Tired. His jowls sagged like a bloodhound's.

"I'm sure the homicide investigators will consider that," Trevor agreed, his gaze wandering once more toward Skye. "But I suspect we know their conclusion."

"Which means we need to step up our search for the guy even more."

Trevor nodded. "Let me know how I can help, Chief," he said, acting the role of the good subordinate officer he was.

But that was not all he was. He'd do everything necessary to stop Marinaro from hurting, or killing, anyone else.

Anything.

Even… Hell, he still wanted to enlist Skye and Bella, the only K-9 on the force who'd most likely gotten the actual scent of Marinaro. Never mind that. It probably didn't matter which scent dog was used, as long as he could get it access to items that had definitely been touched by Marinaro. And he'd still need some better leads on where to get a K-9 to search.

"You all right?" The chief shifted his stance in front of Trevor. "You're looking a little feverish."

Trevor nodded, attempting to put a cool but interested expression on his face. "Just mad we still don't have the guy. But we'll get him."

The captain looked at him oddly. "Don't do anything foolish, Owens. No grandstanding or putting any lives in danger, including your own."

"Yes, sir." Trevor meant it, at least regarding other lives. As for his own, well, he'd do what he had to.

A couple of investigators joined them, and Trevor left the chief talking to them.

The crowd of law enforcement officers was thinning. The media and other onlookers were being held back by crime scene tape and diligent cops.

But Skye was still talking to the same group of guys. Her presence attracted Trevor like some super-charged magnetic force.

Hell, he didn't have to believe what she said, or even think her rational, to want to be near her.

Following his instinct, he approached her. Her beautiful blue eyes watched his every step, even as she continued to converse with those around her.

As he drew closer, he noticed a wariness in her gaze, as if she anticipated he would tell the others about their last meeting, or at least their last conversation.

He gave her a smile that he hoped conveyed some reassurance. All that stuff was strictly between them…just like the way he burned for her.

Noticing him as the dogs stood and started wagging their tails, Ron Gollar and Jim Herman moved aside so he could join the group.

"You're the one here who probably wants more than anyone else to get this guy," Ron said.

"Assuming it really is Marinaro," Jim added.

Manny Igoa, his back toward him, turned to see what got Rusty so excited. "It's gotta be him," he said. "Right, Owens?"

"Yeah." Then, looking straight into Skye's beautiful, concerned face, he asked, "Can I talk to you for a minute?"

He kept himself from wincing at the chilly ambivalence that tautened her features. "Of course," she said, with no warmth, or even inflection. "Later."

She turned back to the others. "We all want to find that bastard Marinaro, but Trevor and I have special reasons—Trevor because he was shot by him, and me because I want Bella to get the credit for finding him. Anyone want to join us for brainstorming when we're off duty?"

None did, which didn't seem to make Skye happy. Maybe she didn't want to be alone with him later. Or ever again.

That sent a pang of hurt through him, which was nearly as painful as the stab in his side from Edinger.

Skye would be off duty long before him, since he didn't officially start his day for another couple of hours. But they set up a time to meet. And a place. In public.

Skye was grateful, in a way, that Trevor chose this particular coffee shop. It was close to her home and that gave her a good reason not to encourage Trevor to pick her up. She didn't want their meeting to seem like a date.

She walked over with Bella. Since they arrived first, Skye chose a quiet table on the fringes of the patron area on the sidewalk and left Bella guarding it while she went inside.

Though she usually preferred strong, black coffee, it was late enough that she didn't want too much caffeine hype. Plus she already felt wired about this meeting.

Instead, she chose a sweet, icy cinnamon mocha. The summer evening was warm enough that it seemed appropriate. When she saw Trevor striding toward the shop in his tight jeans and tighter red knit shirt that spotlighted his chest and bare biceps, her shiver had nothing to do with the coldness of her drink.

He looked so…well, tasty. Especially when he smiled as he saw her.

He bent to pat Bella's head as the K-9 stood and wagged her tail eagerly.

"Hi," Skye said, irritated at herself for wanting to greet him as effusively as Bella just did. She apologized for not getting him anything. "I wasn't sure what you'd want at seven o'clock at night, and something hot might have cooled off by now."

"What I generally want at this hour isn't different from any other time of the day." His words were vague enough, but the way his brown eyes skimmed over her made them a whole lot more suggestive.

No matter what else happened between them, he still seemed to want her. Maybe as much as she wanted him....

She watched his back as he went inside. Especially his tight butt.

Oh, heavens, she had it bad. But she had to concentrate on business—on figuring out how to handle him now that she had revealed the secret of her heritage, which was never to be disclosed to an outsider.

Only...she didn't believe Trevor was a full outsider, especially not now. And if he really did have the power she feared he did, she couldn't avoid talking to him. Being with him. Watching him.

And, if necessary, finding a way to control him.

Yeah, right.

He returned with a large cup with a sleeve and top and pulled the other metal chair from under the small, round table. He lowered himself into it and just looked, for a moment, toward Skye. Then he spoke. "I appreciate your agreeing to meet with me, Skye. I figured it would be awkward to get together tonight. But whatever you think… I mean, if you really believe you can do what you said you do with dying people, or that I can kill by just… Aw, hell. I thought all day about how I'd just be cool and get beyond this belief of yours, but it's not something I can just ignore."

"I don't want you to ignore it, Trevor," Skye said sadly. "And it doesn't even matter if you believe I'm wrong about how Edinger really died and your involvement. But in case I'm right, we need to stay…" Skye paused for a moment as she groped for the right words. "We need to stay friendly." But she wanted more. "If you get into a situation like that again, you have to be careful," she continued. "Maybe even get guidance about how to control your new abilities."

"Guidance from someone who thinks she can either waltz a dying guy over some kind of bridge, or twitch her nose and bring him back to life?" His tone had turned scoffing, though something in his eyes told her he didn't completely disbelieve her. But his attitude hurt.

"Exactly." She forced a smile.

He pulled his gaze away, and when he again looked at her over the table his expression was unreadable. "Look, Skye, maybe there is something to what you said. I realize that my surviving, after being shot the way Marinaro got me, was amazing. You were there. I had hallucinations about seeing Wes Danver after he was shot, too, and a bridge and stuff. And you. But it's all just so, well, weird. Incredible. You have to grant me that."

Skye nodded. He was right. This had to be awfully difficult to buy into for any person who'd never heard of it.

Trevor reached over the table and touched her chin. "I'm sorry, Skye," he said. "If I could fully believe what you said, I would. But I just can't."

"I understand."

"You know how important it is to me to capture Marinaro," he continued. "That's why I'd wanted to enlist Bella and her scenting ability to help me in an investigation separate from the official one."

"Yes, I know." Skye's heart plummeted to her toes. She heard the "but" in his voice. Not that she'd truly believed Bella and she would be able to do much, not without more information on where to track Marinaro. But at least that would give her some reason to stay in close contact with Trevor. She had to be sure he didn't abuse the power she had accidentally given him.

But she knew she was lying to herself. She wanted to be with Trevor, period.

"But—" he said, reaching across the table and taking her hand in his warm grasp. "I need some time to think about all this. It'll be better if I look for Marinaro on my own. Although I'm open to ideas from you."

Bella put her head on Trevor's lap, and he stroked her with the hand not holding Skye's.

He looked back at Skye. "You understand, don't you?"

"Sure." She withdrew her hand and stood up. It felt like she was severing a connection with an irreplaceable part of her life. Nevertheless, she spoke brightly. "Well, it's been a long day. See you around the station."

"Skye—" Trevor was standing now, too, and the expression on his gorgeous features was clearly troubled.

"Take care of yourself, Trevor," Skye said. She pulled on Bella's leash and they quickly walked away.

Chapter 17

Although Skye was exhausted that night, she couldn't sleep. Her beautiful black Bella sensed her sadness and snuggled up with her in bed, but even that didn't help.

Just as she was getting off duty the next night, there was a call-out similar to the one the night before. Yet another young woman had been assaulted and murdered in one of Angeles Beach's less savory neighborhoods. The dispatcher sent officers to the crime scene.

It was not a hostage situation, or other circumstance where SWAT would be involved. Still, even without official SWAT involvement, Skye knew Trevor would be there.

She sped to the crime scene with Bella. When they arrived, Trevor was already deep in conversation with crime scene techs. He nodded a cool greeting to her from down the block. Her insides warmed at the sight of him, even as the distance between them—created by more than how far apart they stood—made her eyes misty.

"You okay, Skye?" Ron Gollar asked. He'd been summoned to work crowd control again.

She pretended that the breeze from the nearby ocean had blown something into her eyes. "Of course," she said briskly. "Any sign of the suspect here?"

"Same calling cards that Marinaro's getting famous for," Ron told her, shaking his head. "You'd think the bastard would do something different."

"At least the last couple of times he hasn't hung around to shoot anyone else," Skye reminded him, giving a tiny tug on Bella's lead. They headed to where her fellow K-9 officers congregated.

This time, most K-9s were present, not just Bella and Rusty. But after being released to carry out their orders, not even one dog picked up a good scent trail, despite sniffing the shell casings and rubber gloves left on the scene.

There were no witnesses, and the crime had been called in by someone uninvolved—a hysterical woman who'd heard shots about an hour ago. She lived in another unit in the seedy apartment complex that was filled with small passageways and innumerable exits.

And Skye arrived much too late to utilize any of her Valkyrie powers to save the victim or help her cross over. She was frustrated and immeasurably sad. So what if the woman's initial ID revealed that she had been arrested for prostitution and drug dealing numerous times? Even had a trial pending. She had been a *person*. Even if the accusations were true, she hadn't deserved to die this way.

Word traveled fast among members of the Angeles Beach Police Department that investigators were considering that this situation, like the last one, could be a copycat crime. But there was no good evidence to support that.

Once more, it appeared, Marinaro had gotten away with murder...for now.

For the next week, Skye went to work, trained with Bella, met with her friends from home for coffee a couple of times and—whenever possible—stalked Trevor.

Oh, it wasn't exactly stalking. Stalking generally involved someone who was either crazy or who wanted to do the victim harm.

And she wasn't crazy, despite what Trevor thought. Nor did she wish him harm.

But she kept him in sight whenever possible. She did practice workouts with Bella in the fenced yard while the SWAT guys did maneuvers. She hung around the station when she knew Trevor would arrive after her. She came in early when he did.

She also came to know the area where he'd bought a condo—a pleasant, midscale area of Angeles Beach that was half a mile from the beach, with plenty of nice shops and restaurants, which he didn't seem to frequent. She sometimes watched him come and go from his place.

Best of all, she kept up with the assignments for which SWAT was called out—or where killers whose crimes might interest Trevor were sought, even if their arrests did not require the extra assistance of SWAT.

Fortunately, there was no indication that Trevor was doing anything more than his duty as one sexy, healthy, skilled SWAT officer. One who always greeted her politely when they got near each other—

occurrences that made Skye sad with their infre-
quency and coolness.

In the meantime, the media reported excitedly on
the latest murders as the department dug into the in-
vestigations and released enough information to
make it clear who their primary suspect was.

Then, early one morning, before all officers
were to convene in the roll call room, Trevor came
up to her in the hallway as she prepared to enter
with Bella.

"Good morning," he said with no inflection. But
just the fact that he was talking to her at all made
Skye's heart race.

"Hello, Trevor." She hoped she only imagined the
tremor in her voice as she looked up into the chiseled,
perfect features of his face.

"How've you been, Skye?" he asked.

"Fine, and you?" How mundane a conversation—
especially when what she wanted to do was throw
herself into his arms and hold on.

"Well enough. Look—" But whatever he'd
intended to say was lost as the mob of officers around
them expanded, carrying them along in the crowd as
the time to start approached.

Skye and Bella were separated from Trevor. After
grabbing a seat, Skye looked around. As always,

Trevor was in the midst of fellow SWAT officers at the back of the room. Skye sighed as she sat and Ron Gollar joined her.

"Any idea what's going on today?" he asked. "I heard rumors that the captain has something big to talk about."

Which he did. In fact, what Captain Boyd Franks reported that morning made Skye shudder.

Trevor's hands curled into tight fists as he listened to the captain.

"We're still looking into the authenticity of the message," Captain Franks said into the microphone at the front of the crowded, silent room. The anger on his face made him appear even older than his early sixties. "But Adrian Dellos forwarded the e-mail to us." Dellos was the TV reporter who was always critical of the ABPD. "It purported to be from Marinaro. Here, let me read it."

He pulled reading glasses from his shirt pocket and adjusted them, then began. "'To Adrian Dellos. Here is some news for you. The cops are playing games with me, but they are going to wish they didn't. I'll show them all very soon who I am, and what I can do when I really get mad.' It's signed J. Marinaro." The captain shook his head, then removed his glasses. "This could be a hoax, but we're looking into it. In case it's genuine, our BOLO for Marinaro is now ratcheted up even more than before. We have to find him before he does whatever it is he's threatening. Get him in custody."

Now more than ever, Trevor planned on taking care of that miserable killer his own way.

But they had to find him first, which meant he had to terminate his efforts to avoid Skye.

Was she crazy? Maybe. He'd tried hard to convince himself that was true. But too often he kept remembering the day he'd been shot.

Had he really been brought back by Skye? He'd seen her—heard her telling him to come back. No doubt about that. Or was there?

And if that part was somehow true, did it mean the rest of what she'd said was, too? Could he will a bad guy to die? Had he done so with Edinger?

Hey, that was a whole lot better than the way he'd been getting rid of killers before they could hurt anyone else. Better for him, anyway.

He'd noticed Skye hanging around the periphery of his life during the past week. He'd wanted many times to go up to her, but he didn't.

When the captain was done and they'd been dismissed, he caught up with Ron Gollar in the hallway.

"What's the SWAT take on Marinaro's message?" the rookie asked. "Any chance of some early recruitment to increase your ranks?"

"You wish," Trevor said with a grin. Ron smiled back. "I thought your first choice was Narcotics."

"Oh, yeah—no doubt about my wanting to put a stop to the sleazes who deal and all. But after watching you guys in action, I'd rather be in SWAT."

"Got it," Trevor said. "I'll let you know if there's any chance of getting you to train with us one of these days so you can show us what you've got. Your military background's a big plus, even though you're still green around here."

"Thanks," Ron said, then hurried off to catch up with his partner.

Trevor looked for Skye. She stood farther down the hall with the other K-9 officers, who also had their dogs with them. He made his way through the lightening crowd. "Can we talk?" he asked when he caught up with her.

A sweet, surprised expression crossed quickly over her face, followed by studied coolness. "Go ahead," she said, without moving from her fellow officers.

"Over here. Please." He gestured toward a corner.

With a shrug, she followed, Bella at her side. "I'm not sure what you and I have to talk about. Unless you're about to tell me you're now certain I'm crazy, and I don't really want to hear that."

He grimaced. But, hell, he wouldn't tell her, here in the middle of everyone, that he'd reflected on her story—and couldn't completely discount it. "No," he told her, "but assuming you're not crazy, that e-mail makes it more critical that we do something, don't you think?"

"We work with a lot of good cops and investigators," she said. "Let's just do our jobs." Was it his imagination, or did her icy tone and curt words conflict with the expression on her face?

Hell, he wasn't much for reading people, but she looked sad and full of longing. Or was he just reading his own emotions into hers?

"All right," he said. "See you around, Skye." But before he turned away, he touched her shoulder. "Count on it."

Another anonymous tip had been phoned in. Reliable? Maybe not, but it had contained enough details that they had to check it out.

As screwy as it sounded, Marinaro had allegedly been spotted at an upscale department store in Angeles Beach's poshest district. It was the middle of the night. The store was closed.

But a young woman who worked there had been reported missing earlier that evening, and her name had been included in the tip.

This could be a hostage situation, and Trevor was ready. *Really* ready, as his SWAT team geared up and got into position.

Was this a trap, the payback Marinaro had threatened in his message to the media? They'd find out soon. The team leader, Carl Shavinsky, held up his gloved hand to signal the guys to get ready. As always on their missions now, Trevor was reminded of Wes Danver. How he had gestured the same way at the warehouse.

And died.

Trevor had a hard time standing still. If Marinaro was here, he would be apprehended this time, dead or alive. And Trevor knew which he preferred.

Like his team members, he aimed his modified AK-47 assault rifle toward the building. He glanced at the crowd of black-and-whites and officers waiting for their orders.

Among them was Skye, Bella at her side. Both wore protective gear.

Trevor wanted to say goodbye, in case this was his last mission. If he was shot this time, could she save him again?

Would she save him?

Right now, with his nerves on alert, he could believe almost anything, including perhaps the fact that he could kill just by commanding the suspect to die.

Once again, the current team leader went in first. No need to bust down this door. The store manager was cooperating fully. A key had been provided, the entry unlocked.

"Angeles Beach P.D.," Carl called, his voice deeper and louder than Danver's had been. "You here, Marinaro? We got you this time."

Again, SWAT officers in protective gear ran in, their small microphones looped in front of their mouths, weapons ready. Their shouts were chaotic in the empty store that was dimly lit only by security lights. "Marinaro? Come out before you get hurt."

Was the tip that had brought them here correct? Had it been from the suspect?

They stalked around display counters, pivoting often to resight their weapons. But they saw no one. Until...

"Hey!" came a shout from Trevor's right, followed by more. "Miss? Hell, she's been shot. Is that him? Marinaro? Drop your weapon! Now! Hell, he's getting away!"

"See to the victim—the female," Carl shouted, running in the direction Marinaro had probably fled.

Trevor moved forward and looked down. Behind a counter lay a beautiful young woman. Her clothing suggested she shopped here often. The amount of blood on her suggested she might have shopped here for the last time.

Rage surged through him. He'd been too late to protect her.

And Marinaro? Could he be getting away—again?

Nothing Trevor could do about that at this moment. He reached down, touched the side of the woman's neck.

A pulse! Very faint, but... Trevor lifted his radio to demand that someone call the EMTs. But first he would call Skye.

No need. "Oh, my, there she is," said a soft, familiar voice from beside him. He looked up. Skye stood there, Bella at her side looking edgy but staying still.

"She's alive," he told Skye. "Barely."

"I know."

"Can you save her?" he demanded.

There it was. The challenge. *Could* she save the woman? If she did, would he have any choice but to believe in the powers she'd professed to have?

He'd figure that out later.

"I'll see, Trevor," she whispered, looking him straight in the eye. "Please distract the others for now."

Other officers had entered the store, going into areas already cleared by SWAT, looking for victims.

A couple officers approached them.

Hell, here goes, Trevor thought. "Stay back," he commanded. "Officer Rydell is an expert on first aid." Was that true? He didn't really know, but it would at least get Skye where she needed to be. "Someone call the EMTs while she sees if she can help the victim."

He watched as she knelt beside the woman. Bella backed off, almost as if she understood what her partner was doing. Skye took the woman's well-manicured hand as she closed her own lovely blue eyes. Her fair skin grew even paler as Trevor watched, and her head nodded slightly, as if in response to a rhythm only she could hear.

He realized some of the other guys were watching, so he stood. "Back off!" he ordered again. "Give them space."

He saw Ron Gollar at the fringe of the officers. Ron nodded slightly as if he knew exactly what was going on. "Over here!" he shouted. "I think I saw a reflection from a weapon—up this escalator!"

Nearly all the officers followed him, checking behind other counters and clothing racks.

Trevor didn't know how much time passed while he watched Skye. A minute? Several? And then the injured woman started to gasp for air.

"Hey, is she okay?" one of the other officers said, and as everyone turned to look Trevor kept them from getting closer.

The EMTs soon arrived and took over from Skye. She rose, looking as weak as if she had handed the woman some of her own life force. Was that how she did it?

He didn't know, but he was going to find out.

He approached and put an arm around her, trying to make it look more like a friendly gesture to a comrade in arms than the hug he intended. "Are you all right?" he whispered.

"I am now." Skye's voice was soft and hoarse. "She wasn't as close as you were, but she could have gone either way." She looked deeply into his eyes. "She's a nice lady. Hardworking. Has a young family and a lot left to do with her life. It only took a moment for me to decide to save her."

Would the woman have survived anyway? Maybe, but Trevor didn't think so. He wanted to hear more. A lot more.

"Good job, Officer Rydell," he told her with a smile. "How about grabbing dinner with me later, when we're off duty?" He waited, unhappy that he felt so nervous about her reply.

"All right, Trevor," she finally said.

And it was all he could do not to kiss her right there.

Marinaro had gotten away through the store's honeycomb of exits and loading docks. The SWAT guys and others had been questioned and reprimanded by their superiors, and then had to cooperate in a press conference where the latest incident was discussed and the cooperation of citizens was requested to find this armed and dangerous suspect.

Dellos had all but taken charge of the inquisition. Skye had gone home and watched it on TV. The guy seemed to love rubbing the ABPD's nose in its failures, especially those regarding Marinaro.

Skye was sure Trevor wouldn't be in the best of moods when he finally joined Bella and her at the outdoor patio of the hamburger joint nearest to the station. But fast and informal was what they both needed now.

She was looking forward to Trevor's admission that she had, in fact, passed the test.

Skye hadn't really minded Trevor's scrutiny as she helped the victim survive. The woman's spirit had already arrived on the rainbow bridge, but she hadn't had to work hard to bring her back. And as she'd told Trevor, her decision had been easy this time. The victim had a loving husband and babies at home. She was a manager at the department store where she'd been attacked, which was why she'd been there so late.

Fortunately, she had described her attacker. Definitely Marinaro. In fact, he'd even given her his name.

"Just so you know," he'd said to her. "Someone's been imitating me. But I'm for real. Too bad you won't be alive to report it—but I'll make sure the damned cops learn their lesson." That had been after the sexual assault... And then he'd shot the woman.

"Hi," said the deep voice Skye was coming to love. She looked up to see Trevor. He wore the gray sweats of the SWAT team training outfit, and he looked exhausted.

As he bent to pat Bella, Skye said, "Sit down and tell me what you want. I'll go get it for you."

"What I want," he told her, standing and drawing her to her feet, "is you."

Much later, Skye looked over toward Trevor. He lay on top of her sheets, breathing hard, with the sexiest grin on his face.

For someone as exhausted as he was, he'd done

wonders, first with his caresses and kisses, which made her nearly crazy with craving him, and then with satisfying her—more than once.

She couldn't help grinning back. Maybe foolishly. But this man did things to her in ways she couldn't explain, even to herself.

She was in love.

But before she could say anything, he reached down and pulled her burgundy-colored sheets over both of them. "Okay," he said, "you convinced me today—although I think I knew the truth even before. And if you can save lives that way, I have to believe your explanation of how I killed Edinger. I need to know how to deal with that power."

She nodded, her hair moving along the pillow where her head lay. "Just be aware of it," she told him. "Be sure you only use it when you have to. I trust you, Trevor. I don't think you'd hurt anyone indiscriminately, but—"

"Not if it made me look bad in your eyes, Skye," he said, bending toward her. As his mouth met hers as it had so many times this night, she shivered in delight as she heard him whisper, "I love you."

And as she told him she loved him, too, he began once more to touch her body intimately, lovingly, exquisitely…and for an additional time that night, she succumbed to the passion of being one with Trevor Owens.

Chapter 18

"And you believed him?" Hayley sounded completely dubious.

Skye sat on the sleek red sofa bed she had picked up at a large chain store that sold mostly Scandinavian products. She held her phone's portable handset up to her ear with one hand as she scratched Bella's tummy with the other. Her favorite classical music CD played softly in the background.

"Yes," she responded quietly. "I believe he won't abuse the power." She'd just told Hayley about how

Trevor helped shield her at the crime scene the previous day.

But she didn't explain that Trevor's promise of caution had been made between phenomenal bouts of lovemaking.

"Well, the whole thing's pretty amazing," Hayley continued. "After all these years dealing with our own abilities, I guess we've seen enough not to discount anything that's supposedly a myth of our culture. But a guy getting any power at all, when we're used to it being a women-only thing? Scary. Especially that kind of power, conveyed without intent but because of a sexual connection." She paused. "So how is he in bed? I assume you're still *connected* to each other that way."

"I'll let you make whatever assumptions you want." Skye felt embarrassed despite the fact that Hayley was one of her oldest friends. Her change in mood must have been obvious to Bella, since the Malinois rolled to a sitting position beside her on the sofa and whined.

"Well, let me know if he has any friends whose lives need to be saved. My love life needs an upgrade."

"Good night, Hayley," Skye said with a laugh, then hung up.

Her timing couldn't have been better. The doorbell rang, and Bella started barking. Skye hurried to answer the door. She knew exactly who stood there, waiting to come in.

She threw the door open and enjoyed the lustful grin he leveled on her. "Hello, Skye," Trevor said in the sexiest tone she had ever heard. His dark, sensual eyes took in her body as if she'd stripped to greet him.

She was immediately engulfed in his arms. His hard body against her curves nearly turned her legs to the consistency of sand.

"Come in," she managed to gasp as his lips engaged hers in one of the hot, sexy kisses she had already come to love.

And he did.

The next week was heavenly beyond Skye's most imaginative dreams. Nothing especially exciting occurred during her times on duty, which didn't always coincide with Trevor's. And when they ran into each other at the station, they behaved with utmost circumspection—though she wanted to jump his bones right there.

But nighttimes… Whenever possible, they spent them together. In her bed, his, it didn't matter.

Skye had fallen for Trevor as hard as a woman could. This had to be the reason she'd felt a connection with him when she had found him dying.

The love they now shared had to be the reason she had been compelled to bring him back.

Everything was wonderful, and Skye was happier than she had ever been.

She knew it was too good to last.

The 911 call had come in about an hour ago—at one o'clock in the morning. SWAT was immediately deployed, since the woman who'd called had whispered that someone was after her. She gave the address of this rambling, three-story warehouse a mile closer to the ocean than the one where Danver had been killed and Trevor wounded. Had it only been six weeks ago? It felt like months to Trevor. A lifetime.

A lifetime changed irrevocably by that night when he was introduced to Skye and her amazing powers.

Powers he now believed in.

Powers he now, perhaps, shared—to some extent.

Along with the other SWAT team members at the scene, Trevor scrambled into his protective gear. They had assembled behind the big black van glistening under the artificial light in the alley, which was now filled with black-and-whites and the officers on duty who would follow SWAT in once they had control of the warehouse.

And the suspect. And, hopefully, a living, breathing, rescued victim.

Trevor heard a screech of brakes and peered around the edge of the van. A vehicle skidded to a stop at the perimeter of the scene. A news van?

"Keep the civilians back!" shouted Shavinsky. Trevor wanted to shout himself, or kick some butt, as Dellos exited the van with a microphone in his hand. Was he already on the air? Trashing the ABPD yet again?

Where were the officers who dealt with crowd control? Trevor didn't see Ron Gollar. A couple of K-9 officers were there, at least, including Manny Igoa and his dog, Rusty. They headed toward the news van, and Trevor heard the loud protestations of Dellos, who was probably on the air so he could claim police interference with First Amendment rights or something equally inflammatory.

But Trevor did not see Skye and Bella. Just as well. There was a lot he shared with her these days. A lot more he wanted to share with her. But now that they were involved—hey, maybe he was being overprotective, but he really hated the idea of Skye threatened by the perils of a crime scene with an unpredictable SOB like Marinaro.

"Hey, Owens, you want to go in with the first

group?" Shavinsky returned to the cover of the van. He was definitely team leader now, though Trevor had not won the office pool about when he'd be permanently appointed. Carl had already suited up and would be among the first to enter. Trevor knew it involved a lot of trust for Carl to ask him to go in with him.

Either that or Carl knew Trevor would do anything to get rid of Marinaro once and for all—by legitimate means, or not.

SWAT, and the entire department, was convinced that this was another of Marinaro's crimes. The victim—a working girl who was into drugs—had been sexually assaulted and murdered.

"Count me in," Trevor said grimly. He was ready. His AK-47 was cradled in his arms, and he was prepared to shoot or, if the situation warranted it, to set his eyes on Marinaro and will him to die. Painfully, if possible.

He looked around. A couple of K-9 cops—Tritt and Vesco—stood behind their vehicles. Presumably, their dogs were beside them, on the ground. Still no Skye, though.

Trevor had promised Skye not to use his new, presumed ability without first considering the consequences. But if he had an opportunity to dispose of Marinaro without anyone else getting hurt—well,

that had been his intent since long before he could
have gained any special abilities from her.

Carl had his radio up to his ear. He looked
pissed, and his tone wasn't too calm, either. Apparently the chief had given him orders to delay
entering.

Did the powers that be think Marinaro was
suddenly going to get scared by the police and give
himself up? That would be as likely as his suddenly
sprouting a halo and wings.

They stood there with their proverbial thumbs up
their behinds for what felt like eternity, but was
probably only ten minutes.

While they were waiting, Trevor saw Skye arrive
with Bella. She maneuvered around the van where
the damned reporter still seemed to be conducting his
blow-by-blow commentary. She looked around anx-
iously until she met his gaze. She still looked
worried, but he smiled as reassuringly as he could at
her from half a block away.

Gunshots! From somewhere inside! And screams.
Female. The victim was still alive? Why were they
still out here?

"Let's do it!" Carl Shavinsky shouted, either over-
riding his orders because of the change in the situation—or getting new and improved orders.

No need to bust the door open. The warehouse was unlocked.

"Angeles Beach P.D.," Carl yelled. "Everyone inside—drop any weapons and come forward with your hands on your head. Now!"

This place was similar to the last warehouse, but the crates on pallets were neat and there was no smell of anything resembling oil or car parts. The labels on the boxes were from large food manufacturers.

But that didn't matter. The massive stacks still provided too many hiding places.

The SWAT team entered. Like Trevor, each sighted along his weapon, aimed, then let up, only to rush forward, pivot and do it again.

No signs of life.

"Hey, miss, are you in here? Marinaro? Who's here?" The place resounded with the team members' shouts.

And then— "Over here! Quick!"

Trevor hurried in the direction of the shout—and gasped in surprise. "Marinaro!"

The suspect was lying on the floor. A semiautomatic was near his outstretched hand.

And there was a bloody hole in his head.

Had Marinaro taken his own life rather than facing the law?

Disappointment flooded through Trevor, even as he realized how foolish that was. Since they'd heard the woman scream, there was hope that she remained alive.

With Marinaro gone, no one else needed to face death that day—including him.

"What the hell happened here?" Carl demanded.

As soon as he got the words out, they heard the woman scream again.

Skye stood absolutely still when the sound of the woman's scream again sliced through the air outside the sprawling warehouse. What was going on inside? Could she help the woman?

Did she need to help Trevor?

She wanted to grab Bella's leash and dash in, but instead she waited. For now.

Because of her ability to save lives, she always kept her department radio on low, even when she was off-duty. She had heard the call-out about forty-five minutes ago and followed it up by turning on the TV news, then threw on her uniform and raced here in her personal car with Bella in the back. Parking at the fringe of the crime scene, she'd grabbed the extra set of protective gear that she now kept in the car for emergencies and dashed to where her fellow officers had massed. She came prepared to help however she was needed.

Almost immediately, she'd heard a scream, gunshots…and distant, nearly inaudible chanting. Someone in that building had been near death. But the chanting had stopped right away. It was too late for Skye to help whoever it was.

It wasn't Trevor, though, thank heavens. As soon as she'd arrived, before the scream, she saw him pacing outside the warehouse, like a dark, sleek panther on the prowl awaiting the chance to leap onto his prey.

Skye was unsure why the SWAT team hadn't immediately accomplished a brute-force entry, but she had caught Trevor's glance before he joined his group in finally storming the warehouse.

She hated waiting under any circumstances, but standing still here, now, was worse than usual. She wanted more than anything to be inside, too. To at least know what was going on. To determine who had died in there. Had Marinaro deviated from his prior scenario by taking more than one female captive to assault and kill? Or had someone else been in the warehouse whom he'd decided to eliminate?

Just then, one of the SWAT guys got on the radio. Skye yanked it from her heavy utility belt and heard

the announcement that they had found Marinaro, and
he was dead.

It might have been his end that had been the cause
of the chanting Skye had heard. Skye was glad she
hadn't been there as he expired. She could guess
where his spirit would end up, and she would not
have chosen to help him peacefully to the other side.

So it was over. Or was it?

Another scream—from a female—made Skye
wince. The same female who'd screamed before?
Probably.

She looked around. Bella and she were surrounded by other law enforcement personnel, all
shouting and swearing and clutching their weapons,
preparing to barge in. The other K-9 officers here,
Tritt and Vesco, were at the other end of the row of
irregularly parked vehicles, and she didn't want to go
toward them. Not yet.

She looked at the edges of the crime scene, toward
where yellow tape was strung to keep out onlookers,
including media jackals like Dellos. Skye couldn't
complain about him too much at this moment,
though, since his sensational commentary had helped
to bring her up to date as she'd hurried here.

Usually, she spotted Ron when he was keeping the
crowd at bay, but she didn't see him now.

And then…shots resounded again from inside. Skye froze, listening for more. For chanting. For anything.

She had to know what was happening. Trevor was in there. What if he was hit again? She had no idea if she could do anything for him, even see him to the other side, if… No! She wouldn't even think about that possibility.

But she had to do something. Now.

Taking only an instant to clear it with a distracted superior officer, she pulled gently on Bella's leash, then led her to the side of the warehouse. Then, with her back to the wall and Bella at her side, she edged along until she found an entrance. The door was unlocked. Had this been the suspect's entry point?

With one hand on her weapon, Skye led Bella inside. The place was illuminated, though dimly, by a row of security lights along the edge of the high warehouse ceiling.

The best way to find anyone was to follow Bella's nose. "Search, Bella," Skye commanded softly, knowing she might just be confusing her partner since she hadn't given her an object to smell first, a scent to lead her.

But Bella put her long, dark nose to the floor and walked forward, down an aisle formed by the crates.

Skye strained to hear anything in the warehouse that would give her a clue about where she'd find another person—preferably the woman who had screamed. If she ran into the SWAT guys, who wouldn't want her here, she'd need to make up a story about how Bella's urgent tugging on her lead outside led Skye to believe that Bella had heard something from inside—the cries of the victim, perhaps. That led Skye to believe she could find the victim more quickly than they could, which might, in fact, be the case.

So what scent was Bella following? Maybe none, for now her head was raised as her pace quickened, and Skye hurried to keep up. Bella's pointed ears twisted alertly as she loped forward. She must be hearing something beyond Skye's range of hearing that got her excited.

And then Skye heard it, too—a woman's voice. Where were the SWAT guys? She grabbed her radio, preparing to call them, but heard the woman whimper, "Please don't hurt me anymore. Just let me go. I won't say anything." The sound came from her right, and she held Bella back as she peered around a corner. The rows of pallets stopped at a doorway that appeared to go into an office.

The woman was in there.

"Shut up, bitch, and let me think," responded a raspy voice. Marinaro's?

But someone on the radio had said he was dead. Was that a ploy to throw them off? Maybe Marinaro himself had stolen a radio and made that announcement.

Something about that voice sounded familiar....

A thump. The woman cried out, softer this time.

"Shut up!" the man shouted again.

Skye grabbed her radio, pushed the button and quietly called for backup, unsure if her explanation of her location would allow anyone to find her quickly.

Then she wrapped Bella's leash around the wooden slats of a pallet. "Stay," she whispered. She wasn't certain what she would find in that room, but she didn't want her partner to get hurt.

She drew her Glock, held it in both hands, positioning it for firing if necessary. She maneuvered carefully so she couldn't be seen through the open doorway and kept her back against the outer wall to the office. She waited, listening. She heard the woman crying, but nothing else.

What was going on in that room? If she waited for her backup to arrive, the victim might be harmed even more, maybe killed. Skye inhaled deeply, readied herself, then pivoted into the open doorway, her weapon aimed. "Angeles Beach

Police," she shouted, hoping that some of the SWAT guys were near enough to hurry to her assistance. "Freeze."

And found herself facing Ron Gollar. Although he wasn't in uniform, he wore a protective vest. He had on latex gloves, and his police-issue weapon, almost the same as her own, was at the ready to fire.

"Ron? Did you already apprehend the suspect?" But she was nearly certain she knew the ominous answer. He *was* the suspect.

"Drop it, Skye," he growled. His tone was throaty, menacing, not at all the sound of her longtime friend.

"What's going on, Ron?" she asked without lowering her weapon. "I don't understand."

"He kidnapped me," shrieked a voice from behind him. "He's going to kill me like he did my friends. He told me so. He already killed that other man."

"That dumb-ass Marinaro showed up." Ron's hands trembled in obvious distress. His face, usually so boyish and sweet, looked drawn. Angry. "Someone saw us come in here and told the damned reporters, who said something on the news." The reporters Skye had heard on her way to the scene had in fact mentioned an unidentified witness who had claimed to have seen suspicious activity around this site—like a woman under duress. "He came here to stop the copycat stuff he was being blamed for. He wanted to kill me—but I got him first."

"I still don't understand." Skye wished she could see more of their surroundings. From what was visible in the periphery of her vision, this was, in fact, an office—a small one, with file cabinets and a metal desk and not much else. Not much room for her to maneuver. Best she could do would be to distract Ron, try to disarm him. But he was intelligent and had always seemed rational and down-to-earth despite envying the powers shared by Skye and her girlfriends. What had happened to him—and when? Why hadn't she realized it before?

"Sure you understand," he shouted. "You and the others have always had the power of life and death, but not me. You even gave power to your lover, Owens. He's an okay guy, you know? He metes out what he calls justice in his own way—acting in supposed self-defense to kill murderers who've gotten off. Making sure they stop hurting other people. I wanted to make a difference that way, too. Only, I didn't go after innocent young women. I went after hookers who push drugs for their pimps, people who harmed others in the first place—like this bitch." He gestured behind him, and Skye dared to look at the woman on the floor. She was barely dressed, and her limbs appeared to be bound. "Assaulting them sexually—hell, that was fun. In my mind, I thanked Marinaro for making that part of the deal. But I didn't intend to get caught. Ever. Not by Marinaro, and definitely not by you, Skye. Oh, Lord, what am I going to do now?" His voice fell into a wailing whisper.

Skye wished she could hug him. Soothe her longtime friend. She knew he particularly hated drug dealers, thanks to the loss of his friend in high school. But this? He must have felt more than jealousy against Skye and her female friends to take such joy in assaulting and killing women.

Well, first things first. She had to figure out how to help them both out of this potentially no-win situation, then get him the help he needed.

Skye heard stirring in the hallway behind her. Her backup must have finally arrived. But that meant Ron could be in danger. She had to save her friend, help him get past this awful time in whatever way she could.

"I know what you're thinking," Ron continued sadly. "There's no way out for me now. Shoot me, Skye. Then do your magic and help me die peacefully and end up in Valhalla or wherever—the good place. Don't bring me back. I can't live, you know. I can't go to prison."

She couldn't shoot Ron. If he died here, could

she help him over the bridge to a peaceful forever, or would he immediately go to hell?

She hated the sad yet manic look in his pale blue eyes. It hurt her to look at them.

"What the hell's he talking about?" the woman on the floor demanded. Since she wasn't in danger, at least not for now, Skye ignored her.

"We'll see how we can work this out, Ron," she said gently. "I'll do everything I can to help you."

"Then kill me!" His shout reverberated in her mind.

"No," she said sadly. "You know I can't."

She heard a noise from behind her, and Bella dashed in. Her leash was still attached to her collar. Had someone in the hall loosened her to create a diversion, or had she broken free?

No matter. The beautiful black canine was trained to protect Skye as well as scent out suspects. But as she leaped in Ron's direction, she seemed to hesitate in confusion.

"Bite!" Skye ordered, hoping she could grab the gun in Ron's hand without causing him to shoot. But even before Bella got to him, he shot at her. The sound was deafening.

With a yelp, Bella stopped midleap and fell to the concrete floor, whimpering. Bleeding.

"No! How could you do that?" Skye shouted, then

tried to calm herself as she rushed to her dog's side. The shot had missed Bella's protective vest, hitting her at the top of one leg, fortunately only grazing her. Skye looked up and saw that the bullet was embedded in the office wall.

"Kill me," Ron said again, more calmly. "Or I'll shoot her again, and you, too."

"You know I won't do that," Skye told him as she hugged Bella.

"Then get ready." But Ron wasn't looking at her, despite aiming his weapon in her direction. Instead, he looked beyond her. Toward the doorway. "I'll kill her," he said again, matter-of-factly.

Skye knew whom she would see if she turned around.

Sure enough, there was Trevor in the foreground, other SWAT officers behind him. His AK-47 was aimed at Ron.

"Don't hurt him!" she commanded Trevor.

But before she could finish, she heard the thunderous report from Ron's Glock...and pain shot through her upper body.

"Please. Don't—" she tried to say, looking with horror toward Trevor as she fought to stay conscious.

Chapter 19

"Skye!" Trevor yelled as he kept his weapon pointed at the bastard who'd shot her.

He wanted to throw himself onto the floor, shield her from further harm. The shot seemed to have hit her square in her protective vest. She'd hurt like hell, but she'd be okay…wouldn't she?

"I'm okay. Don't hurt him." She was breathing heavily, but since she moved a little and cradled her whimpering dog, he figured she would survive. "You promised."

But he wanted to do something slow, painful—and fatal—to Gollar for what he had done to her.

Still, he *had* promised her…something. Not to become an ineffectual wuss, though. Only to be judicious in his use of the power she had supposedly imparted to him.

Besides, he had an audience—his team members were champing at the bit to get involved. But they wouldn't move until he gave them orders.

"Drop your weapon now," Trevor commanded in a tone that meant business. He kept his AK-47 aimed squarely at the man who had been his fellow cop. The man who'd started to become a friend and was now the worst of enemies.

He had to act fast and get Skye help despite her protestation.

"I'll shoot her again," Ron said. "Unless you kill me." His face was nearly white and there was a madness in his eyes.

Instead of shooting Skye, he aimed at Trevor. The blast reverberated again in the small room. The shot got Trevor's upper arm—making him drop his weapon.

"Kill me—you know how." Ron smiled almost angelically toward Skye. "It's how I want to go. And you know you want to use it."

Trevor had made a promise to Skye, but this guy was obviously a maniac. The only other way of stopping

Ron would be to move out of the way fast and let the sharpshooters behind him take the suspect down.

He prepared to do that. Skye seemed to understand what he was thinking. "Can't we help him?" she pleaded.

"Do it!" Ron shouted. "Or I really will kill her." He again aimed his weapon toward Skye. Toward her head.

No time to see if his team could react fast enough. "Die, then, you bastard!" Trevor yelled at him. "Die. Now. You hear me? Die!" He repeated the command yet again, praying it was enough and that he really did have a special power.

Trevor lunged just in case, ready to take any bullets the SOB shot—only to see Gollar's face grow paler.

Skye screamed and Gollar's body fell lifelessly to the floor.

As she crawled toward the man who had been her friend, Skye knew that the sounds echoing in her mind were not the chanting she always heard when faced with the dying.

"Ron?" she whispered brokenly. She held his limp hand, closed her eyes and sought out his presence on the rainbow bridge so she could at least try to help him in that way.

To no avail. His spirit wasn't there.

He hadn't died as mortals usually did. Indirectly, she had caused his death, and her forebears knew it. Their keening chant was even more mournful than usual, filled with desolation and grief.

She knew that, wherever his spirit had fled, he would not live forever in the halls where his ancestors and innocents dwelled. She hated that idea. Was there nothing she could do?

She began to cry, her sobs blending in her mind with the wails of her ancestresses.

One of their own had been struck down—and as the result of what *she* had created in a stranger.

No—not a stranger. Trevor. The man to whom she'd felt instantly connected.

She had known at that moment that he had something left to accomplish. To be her lover? The man with whom she would share her life? That was what she had come to believe so briefly, notwithstanding the power she had imparted to him.

Even then, even knowing of his personal, violent quest for justice, she hadn't assumed that the reason he demanded to live, the destiny he had yet to accomplish, would be something she would hate. Would despise.

Had he survived just to do what he had done here, today?

To use his power to kill someone she cared about?

Just then, Trevor came over and knelt beside her. He put his arm around her and held her close.

"Is the victim okay?" she asked.

"The EMTs have her. Looks like she'll be all right."

Skye realized that the small room had become crowded with medics and crime scene investigators. One guy bent over Ron, touching his throat, checking his wrist for a pulse.

"And Bella?" she demanded, starting to inch toward her dog, who had moved away and was sitting up now. There was blood on the floor near her, but she did not appear badly injured.

Tritt was with her, looking her over. The older K-9 officer appeared relieved as he glanced toward Skye. "Looks like she was just grazed. I'll get her right to the vet."

"Thanks," Skye said in relief. She wished she could go along, but protocol would require that the EMTs look at her and take her to the hospital for further evaluation.

Trevor had promised her... Technically, he had kept his promise. The power over life and death that she had inadvertently given him—he had used it wisely. To save her life.

But he had nevertheless used it to kill someone she had cared for, deeply.

Something had snapped in Ron. He had apparently craved power over life and death, too. And assumed his own perverted form of justice. Expressed his jealousy, and hatred of women. Awful, yes. But he still shouldn't have died so terribly.

Could she still hope he'd have a peaceful existence afterward? Why hadn't she been able to help him? Couldn't she help him now?

"Okay, miss. Your turn. I understand you were shot." One of the EMTs, a young lady, was bending over her.

"I'm fine," Skye said, ignoring the pain in her chest.

She glanced up toward Trevor, then closed her eyes and lost consciousness.

The chanting sounded far in the distance. Skye listened as it grew closer. She still couldn't understand any words, but she felt one with it.

This time, the chanting was for her. She had willed herself here.

She opened her eyes. She stood on the rainbow bridge. Alone. She still wore her protective police garb, or at least a shimmering semblance of it.

Could she cross the bridge by herself? She had to try. Maybe she had been wrong. Even if she had heard a lamentation instead of supportive chanting, even if she'd had no vision of the rainbow bridge, maybe Ron was there, on the other side.

She had to hope, despite her belief otherwise.

Maybe he was going to be with those who crossed over with the assistance of Skye and her Valkyrie sisters and ancestors.

Please let that be so! she begged silently as she walked forward, surprised that the bridge felt so solid beneath her feet. Before it had always seemed the consistency of water. Smelling something sweet, she headed toward where a light shone so brightly that it obscured what was beyond it.

The sad keening had stopped.

Was that a castle's turret she saw glistening in the brilliance? A church spire?

She had to go see for herself.

Hearing something behind her on the bridge, she turned. Was that Hayley she saw approaching? And Kara? "No!" she called to them. "Stay away!" She pivoted and started hurrying toward the light.

"You must not go on," said a distinct female voice from somewhere within the glow. "You know that, Skye. It is not your time."

Skye knew that voice. It was clear and melodic. One of those who chanted to her?

Her eyes hurt as she strained to see into the illumination and fix it in her mind so she could remember it all—just in case what the voice said was true and she could not continue on.

"I need to make sure that Ron is all right," Skye explained as she took another, tentative step.

"You know better, my dear. He had choices to make, and he opted for the wrong ones. That was why we wept for him. And why you could not help him join us for eternity."

A willowy female figure appeared at the edge of the light. With all the luminosity around her, Skye had a hard time making out her features. She seemed to be dressed in cloudlike vapor. Her hair was almost as pale as her surroundings.

And her face? Hazy, too. Yet she looked vaguely like Skye. Like her mother, and her grandmother, too.

"Yes, I am one of those who came before you," she said in accented English. "And I know you and those of your generation are less accepting of what you are told of your heritage. You ask too many questions." She seemed to smile. "I cannot tell you all. And when you go back to where you belong, you will only have a vague recollection of what you experience here. It will seem dreamlike, as it should. But let me assure you that those who cross this bridge and do not return are at peace. The stories of Valhalla that are shared among your family have some truth to them, and many souls could attest to that."

"But Ron," Skye persisted. "He's not there? What happens to his soul?"

"It has gone...elsewhere. But if he truly regrets what he has done, he might be sent back for another chance."

"Reincarnation?" Skye asked. "And Valhalla? And other legends—they're real?"

She received no answers. The woman's appearance seemed to evaporate slowly as the light surrounding her began to fade. No more shimmering towers beyond her. And the bridge at Skye's feet started to lose substance.

"Skye! Wake up! Come back!" Two different female voices shouted in her mind. "It's not your time. Open your eyes."

But she wasn't ready. Still had no true answers. Wanted—

"Please, Skye, come back to me." This time the voice was deep. Masculine. Trevor.

And she did.

"Welcome back," said Hayley. She was clad in a white medical jacket. Her pretty face was damp and her light blue eyes were bloodshot, as if she had been crying. She bent down and gave Skye a big hug. "You had me damned scared."

"Yeah, I was with the EMT team that first got into that place," Kara Woods said. Her strong-featured face was somber, almost angry. "But most people don't, er…well, avoid our help when we try to do—you know."

Skye did know. She looked around. She had already realized that she lay in a hospital bed, with white sheets drawn up to her chest. Her clothes had been exchanged for a standard, faded aqua hospital gown.

And her friends' circumspection in what they said told Skye that they weren't alone. She turned slightly and realized that a nurse stood beside her, fussing over an IV that dripped something into the back of her hand.

She rolled her eyes as she looked back at her friends. "You don't want to get dehydrated," Hayley chided. "But if you need something for pain—"

"I'm fine," Skye assured them, her voice hoarse but strong. Physically she did feel fine. Emotionally? Well, she was drained. She recalled her visit to the rainbow bridge, seeing Hayley and Kara, and the woman she had spoken with…but it was hazy. Fading.

What she focused on, though, was Trevor. Where was he? She'd heard him. Or had she imagined it?

She hated that he had willed Ron to die that way.

Maybe he'd felt he had no choice. But the pain caused by what he had done, her self-blame for what had happened to Ron and the lack of time to help him regain a grip on reality was agonizing. But no medication could alleviate this pain.

She looked around. "Trevor?" she asked.

"He came to see you, then left when you started to stir," Kara said. "I suspect he thought he wouldn't be welcome."

"When can I get out of here?" she asked.

"You should stay overnight for observation," the nurse said.

"But if you want to go, I'll be leaving in about an hour," Hayley said, "and I can stay with you this evening to make sure you're all right."

"Yes," Skye agreed. "That's what I want to do."

She glanced at Kara, who also nodded. "I'll be glad to keep an eye on you, too," she said.

"So was it real, or were you hallucinating?" Kara demanded, running one hand through her hair in obvious frustration. She was now clad in a snug white T-shirt that showed off her curvaceousness and black denim jeans.

They were back in Skye's home, sitting in her living room. They had ceded the red sofa bed to her and were sitting on the sleek wood-framed chairs with pink pillows. They had helped themselves to a glass of wine from Skye's supply, but they refused to allow her anything stronger than fruit juice.

"I have no idea," Skye said. "The woman who spoke with me—I've no idea if she could have been real. I have this image that she resembled…well, me!"

"So you still can't say for sure who does the chanting we hear, or what the afterlife looks like?" Hayley, too, was no longer dressed for work and had put on a light green button-down shirt that she tucked into jeans. Her light hair looked as limp and exhausted as the rest of her.

Skye had been too tired to change into anything other than her blue ABPD uniform. She'd shower and get ready for bed once she could convince her friends that she was all right and didn't need them to stay overnight. She wanted to be alone.

But not totally alone. She had talked to Tritt, who'd rushed Bella to the veterinarian. Fortunately her dog's wound had not been serious, and she would be returned home within the hour.

"I want to say that what I saw, what I remember of it, was real," Skye said, then sighed and took a sip of the iced cran-apple juice from the glass on the sleek wooden coffee table in front of her. She returned it to the coaster. "The woman...well, she felt real. I identified with her, as if she was my great-something grandmother. My ancestress, in any event. She said my recollection of what I saw and felt would fade, and it has some, already. But the way she described what was beyond, at the end of the bridge—and what would happen to Ron—it all seemed so real at the time."

"Then Ron may not be punished forever?" Kara asked eagerly.

Skye shook her head. "Assuming I wasn't just delirious." She sighed. "On some level, I know why Ron felt he had to do what he did. And we knew he admired Trevor's determination to mete out justice his own way. But Ron, well, his decisions were based on anger and hatred of women, I guess. Us. He carried his version of justice much too far."

Skye had hesitated over Trevor's name. Maybe he'd been there, in the hospital with her, but he'd left. Maybe she'd just imagined him calling her back. And if he had, it might just have been due to his feelings of guilt for how this had ended up.

She had to acknowledge to herself, if not to Trevor, that even if she hated what he'd done and how he made her indirectly responsible for Ron's death, he had done what he thought was needed to save her life.

She understood that. But how could she live with it? And how could she deal with seeing Trevor in the future, when every time she looked at him she would remember what he'd done?

"Ron didn't just skirt the law to achieve his perverted goals," Skye continued sorrowfully. "He raped and killed."

"He went after drug-dealing prostitutes," Hayley said belligerently. "Those women were hurting others, at least by their pushing drugs." She stopped, looked at Kara, then Skye, and sighed. "Hell, we all knew Ron was envious of our life-and-death abilities. Maybe we should have realized how much. What he did was horrible. Unforgivable. But maybe, if we'd understood what was going on with him, we could have prevented what he did."

"I should have guessed what was going on with him," Skye said sadly. "A while back, there was talk about some of the guys helping detectives check on phone messages to Marinaro. I think Ron got involved, so he might have gotten the idea for his own copycat killings then, with the idea he could blame them on Marinaro, with enough detailed information about Marinaro to make the allegations stick.... I just don't know. And then, once, Bella got so confused at a crime scene. I suppose she picked up Ron's scent and not Marinaro's."

"Don't blame yourself," Hayley said staunchly. "That wasn't enough to figure out what Ron was up to."

Skye sighed. "Maybe. But this has all been...well, awful. I think I'll go to Minnesota for a while. Talk to my mother, and both of yours, and some of the others. Get their opinions on how genuine what I learned was—about our powers, and about the other side, and...well, everything. And maybe I'll get a little extra TLC."

"Good idea, kid," Kara said. "Give me enough notice, and I'll try to come along."

"Me, too," Hayley agreed. "Now, why don't you get some sleep? We'll just camp out here for the night."

"I'll get some sleep," Skye agreed, "but I want you both to leave. I really appreciate your being there for me, but right now I need to be alone."

"No way," Kara said.

Hayley stood, obviously ready to protest, too, but the doorbell rang.

"Must be Tritt with Bella," Skye said. "With her here, I'll be fine. Honest."

She was half right. Hayley went into the hall outside the living room to answer the front door, and as Skye heard her talking to someone, Bella bounded into the room and onto her lap. Her right hind leg was bandaged, but otherwise she appeared fine as she started to give Skye canine kisses right on the face.

When Skye laughingly moved her to the side to thank Tritt, she saw it wasn't her K-9 cohort who stood in the doorway to the living room.

It was Trevor.

"Hey," Hayley said, "I think you're right. It's time for Kara and me to go home."

Skye opened her mouth to protest, to invite them to stay the night after all, but it was too late.

Chapter 20

"Hello, Skye," Trevor said softly, not moving from the doorway even when Bella returned to him and nuzzled his legs.

Now that he was here, he wasn't sure what to say. He knew what he wanted to *do*—take her into his arms and never let go.

He'd thought he had lost her.

Hell, he *had* lost her. But at least she was still alive. He'd done what he had to in order to save her even though it meant killing her friend.

"Come in, Trevor," she finally said, her voice as

melodic as always yet with a layer of frost on it. "We need to talk, and now is as good a time as ever."

He didn't need any further invitation. He strode toward the sofa. She looked so pale sitting there on the bright-colored upholstery. Her skin was white and drawn, and all the light shades of her hair seemed to be washed out as it lay askew on her shoulders.

But she had never looked more beautiful to him.

He had thought a lot, in the last few hours, about what to say to her.

She didn't rise to greet him, so he stood there awkwardly for a minute.

And then he sat beside her on the sofa. Bella must have sensed the tension, for she joined them, sitting so her body squeezed between their two pairs of legs, her dark head and shining nose a contrast with the red of the sofa where she rested it. She looked first at Skye, and then at him, as if wondering what was wrong, what would come next.

So did Trevor.

Skye obviously wasn't going to make this easy on him. But, hell, there was nothing he could say to make what had happened go away.

All he could do was let her know how he felt. And if she threw it back in his face?

He'd live with it. He had to.

"I'm sorry for what happened, Skye. For what *had* to happen. I know you didn't want me to do what I did to Ron. I didn't want it, either. But what I did want was for you to live, and if that meant you hated me, then that was how it would be. He said he'd shoot you and aimed at your head, damn it!" He realized he'd started yelling and stopped, taking a deep breath and looking searchingly into her lovely blue eyes. Did he see a hint of thawing, or was it only his wishful imagination? "And then after, when I thought you died..." This time, his voice cracked. Hell, he wasn't a wimp. He wasn't going to get all teary. He wouldn't let himself—especially now, when he knew she was, in fact, all right.

"Would you like to know what happened?" she asked softly.

"Yeah, I would."

Looking at Bella, and not at him, she related a story—of being on the rainbow bridge, of running ahead when Hayley and Kara came to help her, and of what the kind woman who may have been her ancestor told her.

Not long ago, he'd have assumed this was a story she'd made up or that had come to her while unconscious.

Now he accepted it as he accepted her and the

power she had so unintentionally given to him. That power allowed him to preserve her awesome, wonderful life.

"Then, well, whatever happened to Ron, it isn't necessarily for eternity?" He allowed himself a small, relieved grin. He hadn't hated the guy. In fact, he even felt a little sorry for him, the way he'd gone over the edge of sanity.

"It isn't necessarily for eternity," Skye confirmed softly. "But I don't think we'll ever know for sure."

"I was afraid for you," he admitted. "I didn't know what was happening, but when you were still unconscious in the hospital..." He stopped and took a breath. "I knew by then that what you'd told me was real. I wanted to tell you so, even tried to—but your friends were there. You didn't need me. So I just left."

"I heard you," she said.

"You did?" He stared at her.

She nodded. "You called me back."

"And that's why you woke up?"

"Could be," she admitted.

"Hey, this connection stuff—could be a good thing." He smiled. And then he reached over Bella and drew Skye into his arms. She didn't resist.

When she kissed him back as fiercely, as heatedly,

as he kissed her, Trevor wanted to cheer…until the heat of his desire for her obliterated everything else from his mind.

He picked her up and carried her down the hallway to her bedroom. "See you in a while, Bella," he said as he kicked the door shut before the dog, wagging her tail, could follow them in.

Was she crazy? Yes, Skye thought, but as she writhed in her bed while Trevor touched her intimately, she observed his lusciously male body and stroked him back. Skye appreciated how gentle yet erotic Trevor's touches were, obviously taking into account her remaining soreness from the shot against her protective vest. She, in turn, was very much aware of his wound, and was careful not to hurt him.

She gasped as he entered her. He made her feel alive. And wanton. And she wanted him as she had never thought she could want a man.

She gave in to sensation, heat and need and the most ferocious and delicious sexiness she had ever experienced.

When it was over, they lay curled up in each other's arms. Skye reveled in Trevor's heavy breathing and the feeling of his rough, moist skin still touching hers all over. She smiled, savoring the moment.

This was why she had felt compelled to save him.

And why he must have felt compelled to save her.

They were connected. By sex? Yes. But Skye knew it was much more than that. They touched each other in so many ways....

She opened her eyes to find him looking at her, his dark mahogany eyes conveying emotions she had only dreamed about. "I love you, Skye," he said softly. "Could be you bewitched me with those Valkyrie powers of yours. Maybe that's how you gave me my new ability. But I don't care. And I promise I'll never—"

She reached up and put her fingers on his mouth to shush him. "Don't make promises you can't keep. But I love you, too. And we'll be a team from now on."

Epilogue

The next few weeks could not have been more blissful. On the nights Trevor and she both were off duty, he spent them with her, or they went to his place.

When they were on duty, they also tried to work together, as much as possible. Skye was aware of Trevor's growing interest in the case of a violent serial killer who was loose in nearby L.A. The person at the top of the LAPD's suspect list was a guy who'd allegedly committed similar killings in San Bernardino. He'd been apprehended, but was set free after alleged prosecutorial misconduct resulted in a mistrial.

And now the guy had apparently come to Angeles Beach, since killings using the same M.O. had started to occur. He'd park at the side of a road and pretend his car was broken down. When someone stopped to help, he'd rob them and then kill them with their own vehicles. He was too smart to leave prints, but one victim in San Bernardino had survived. So had one, just recently, in L.A.

They weren't all the ABPD's jurisdiction, but maybe that was a good thing, for Skye and Trevor had a plan.

They were a team now. And they knew the kinds of remote roads, near affluent areas, where the suspect was inclined to commit his crimes.

"Do you think it'll be tonight?" Skye asked as they cruised the winding, mountaintop street that they'd selected for occasional stakeouts. This was their third time here. Nothing had happened on the first two nights—except they'd made out like teen-agers while stopped at one end of their surveillance area. If nothing else, they were having fun. Skye left Bella at home on these nights so she could not be hurt.

"We'll see." Trevor drove slowly. "Hey, look over there."

He pointed toward where two cars were stopped on the shoulder ahead. Almost as soon as he did, Skye heard familiar chanting in her head.

"Someone's badly hurt there," she gasped. "Dying."

"Let's do it," Trevor said grimly, pulling quickly off to the side. "Stay safe, Skye."

"You, too," she managed to say as her head spun with the sounds.

They exited the car, weapons drawn. "Police!" Trevor shouted.

The report of a gunshot reverberated along the hillside, and they threw themselves to the ground. Trevor shot out the tires in both vehicles, then they approached, weapons drawn.

"Stay there, or I'll shoot this guy," yelled a male voice from the vicinity of the first car.

"Oh, I'd say you've already done that," Trevor shouted. He glanced at Skye, who nodded grimly.

"I've got to get to the victim right away," she said.

"We're in accord here?"

"Do it."

"You've got one chance," Trevor shouted. "Drop your weapon, shove it this direction, lie facedown on the ground, hands on your head, and we'll take you into custody. Otherwise, you won't survive this night."

Another shot resounded.

"Okay, then. Die, you son of a bitch," Trevor said, inching forward.

Skye got a glimpse of the guy pointing the weapon

at them. Trevor obviously saw him, too, since he aimed his Glock at the same time she aimed hers—no special SWAT weapons tonight.

"You heard me," Trevor shouted. "Die. Right now. Die!"

The suspect suddenly grabbed his chest, gave a yell as if in pain…and fell to the ground, dropping his weapon.

As Trevor carefully edged forward to check on him, Skye advanced toward the front car. The chanting in her mind grew louder, and she silently conveyed her thanks to the ancestress she believed she had met a few weeks earlier on the rainbow bridge.

On the ground beside the car lay a man. Facedown. Carefully, Skye turned him over. He was still breathing, but barely.

She closed her eyes, and suddenly she was on the rainbow bridge with him. The texture where her feet stood was as unsteady as flowing water, but she faced the victim. Her analysis of him, his past and future, was instantaneous, as was her decision. She would save him.

"It is not your time to die," she told him as she glanced toward the light at the far end of the bridge. She saw nothing, no shimmering towers, no Valkyrie forebears to communicate with her. She had been told the vision would fade in her memory, and it had, somewhat. She remained uncertain how much had been her own hopeful subconscious, and how much was true.

But now she had a job to do.

"Come back with me, sir," she said softly to the spirit of the man whose body she had left waiting on the ground by the car. "Your family and friends will be glad you survived this terrible night."

"Thank you." The man had thinning brown hair, a round face and glasses. He looked confused but took the hand Skye offered.

Suddenly she was back, beside the car. The man lay there moaning.

"I've called 911." Trevor put his hand down to help her to her feet.

"The suspect?"

"Gone. Permanently. And I'm sure you didn't see him on your bridge, did you?"

Skye shook her head. She smiled up into Trevor's handsome, beaming face.

"We make a hell of a good team." He lowered his mouth to hers.

* * * * *

ALEXANDROS KAREDES, SNOW DUSTING the shoulders
of his leather jacket and glittering like jewels in his
dark hair, stood at the door. Maria felt the blood drain
from her head.

"Good evening, Ms. Santos."

His voice was as she remembered it. Deep.
Husky. Perfect English, but with the faintest hint
of a Greek accent. And cold, as cold as it had been
that awful morning she would never forget, when
he'd accused her of horrible things, called her
terrible names....

"Aren't you going to ask me in?"

She fought for composure. Last time they'd faced
each other, they'd been on his turf. Now they were
on hers. She was in command here, and that meant
everything.

"There's a sign on the door downstairs," she said,

her tone every bit as frigid as his. "It says, 'No soliciting or vagrants.'"

His lips drew back in a wolfish grin. "Very amusing."

"What do you want, Prince Alexandros?"

A tight smile eased across his mouth and it killed her that even now, knowing he was a vicious, arrogant man, she couldn't help but notice what a handsome mouth it was. Chiseled. Generous. Beautiful, like the rest of him, which made him living proof that beauty could, indeed, be only skin deep.

"Such formality, Maria. You were hardly so proper the last time we were together."

She knew his choice of words was deliberate. She felt her face heat; she couldn't help that but she damned well didn't have to let him lure her into a verbal sparring match.

"I'll ask you once more, your highness. What do you want?"

"Ask me in and I'll tell you."

"I have no intention of asking you in. Tell me why you're here or don't. It's your choice, just as it will be my choice to shut the door in your face."

He laughed. It infuriated her but she could hardly blame him. He was tall—six two, six three—and though he stood with one shoulder leaning against the door frame, hands tucked casually into the pockets of the jacket, his pose was deceptive. He was strong, with the leanly muscled body of a well-trained athlete.

She remembered his body with painful clarity. The feel of him under her hands. The power of him moving over her. The taste of him on her tongue.

Suddenly, he straightened, his laughter gone. "I have not come this distance to stand in your doorway," he said coldly, "and I am not going to leave until I am ready to do so. I suggest you stand aside and stop behaving like a petulant child."

A petulant child? Was that what he thought? This man who had spent hours making love to her and had then accused her of—of trading her body for profit?

Except it had not been love, it had been sex. And the sooner she got rid of him, the better.

She let go of the doorknob and stepped aside. "You have five minutes."

He strolled past her, bringing cold air and the scent of the night with him. She swung toward him, arms folded. He reached past her, pushed the door closed, then folded his arms, too. She wanted to open the door again but she'd be damned if she was going to get into a who's-in-charge-here argument with him. She was in charge, and he would surely see a tussle over the ground rules as a sign of weakness.

Instead, she looked past him at the big clock above her worktable.

"Ten seconds gone," she said briskly. "You're wasting time, your highness."

"What I have to say will take longer than five minutes."

"Then you'll just have to learn to economize. More than five minutes, I'll call the police."

Instantly, his hand was wrapped around her wrist. He tugged her toward him, his dark-chocolate eyes almost black with anger.

"You do that and I'll tell every tabloid shark I can contact about how Maria Santos tried to buy a five-hundred-thousand-dollar commission by seducing a prince." He smiled thinly. "They'll lap it up."

* * * * *

What will it take for this billionaire prince
to realize he's falling in love with his mistress...?
Look for
BILLIONAIRE PRINCE, PREGNANT MISTRESS
by Sandra Marton.
Available July 2009 from Harlequin Presents®.

We'll be spotlighting a different series every month throughout 2009 to celebrate our 60th anniversary.

Look for Harlequin® Presents in July!

THE ROYAL HOUSE *of* KAREDES

TWO CROWNS, TWO ISLANDS, ONE LEGACY
A royal family, torn apart by pride and its lust for power, reunited by purity and passion

Step into the world of Karedes beginning this July with

BILLIONAIRE PRINCE, PREGNANT MISTRESS
by
Sandra Marton

Eight volumes to collect and treasure!

REQUEST YOUR FREE BOOKS!

2 FREE NOVELS PLUS 2 FREE GIFTS!

▼ Silhouette®

nocturne™

Dramatic and Sensual Tales of Paranormal Romance.

SN09

COMING NEXT MONTH

Available July 4, 2009

#67 WILD WOLF • Karen Whiddon
The Pack

There's a new wolf in town, and it's up to Simon Caldwell
to assess the threat. To his shock, the female, Raven,
is young and undeniably attractive. When he is ordered
to exterminate her, Simon knows he must befriend and
protect her. But can a wild wolf be tamed by love?

#68 THE HIGHWAYMAN • Michele Hauf
Wicked Games

Feared in the paranormal realm, the Highwayman kills
demons as well as their conduits—familiars. But it is the
demon he harbors within his own soul that plagues him
the most. As a familiar, Aby Jones would normally be on
his hit list, but he suspects she may be his salvation in
more ways than one....

SNCNMBPA0609